MW01128871

PRAISE FOR THE NOVELS OF

KAREN FENECH

{GONE} Karen Fenech's GONE is a real page turner front to back. You won't be able to put this one down!" —NEW YORK TIMES BESTSELLING AUTHOR KAT MARTIN

{GONE} "Karen Fenech tells a taut tale with great characters and lots of twists. This is a writer you need to read." —USA TODAY BESTSELLING AUTHOR MAUREEN CHILD

{GONE} Readers will find themselves in the grip of GONE as this riveting tale plays out. GONE is a provocative thriller filled with a roller coaster ride that carries the suspense until the last page." —DEBORAH C. JACKSON, ROMANCE REVIEWS TODAY

{BETRAYAL} "An excellent read." —DONNA M. BROWN, ROMANTIC TIMES MAGAZINE

{IMPOSTER: The Protectors Series - Book One} "IMPOSTER is romantic suspense at its best!" —USA TODAY BESTSELLING AUTHOR MAUREEN CHILD

{UNHOLY ANGELS} "... a superbly intricate tale of greed, power, and murder... a suspenseful and believable story that will keep you reading into the wee hours of the morning. Highly recommended! — BESTSELLING AUTHOR D.B. HENSON

NOVELS BY KAREN FENECH

PURSUED

The Protectors Series – Book Three

KAREN FENECH

For Andrew

CHAPTER ONE

He was waiting for her outside the clinic. Shelby had no sooner stepped off the crumbling stoop of the faded, pre-second world war building and into the murky light of the one working street lamp when a man grabbed her from behind. She dropped her purse and briefcase onto the sidewalk that was littered with rotting garbage. She managed a startled shriek before he hooked her at the neck, cutting off her voice and his arm clamped around her waist, crushing her against his body.

Shelby clawed at her attacker's arm. The man wore a light overcoat in deference to the nip in the air on the August night and her attempt to dig her nails into him was futile. She kicked back, striking him in the knee with the heel of her dress pump. He hissed in pain then his grip tightened, squeezing her windpipe like a vise. She'd thought she couldn't breathe before, but now she couldn't take in any air at all.

No ... No!

In her mind she shouted that to him, but in reality she wasn't capable of making any sound other than desperate gasps for air.

Her attacker began dragging her down the sidewalk. She dug her heels into the cracked cement in an attempt to slow him down, but he was stronger and the dim light faded as they left the short street and entered the alley behind the clinic.

"Got a message for you," the man said.

Shelby froze as a new and entirely different fear rose within her.

He brought his lips to her ear. "Tick. Tock."

She didn't need to ask who the message was from. Her insides quivered. She whimpered.

"Hey! You, there! What you doin' to that woman?"

Shelby knew that voice. It was Joseph, the elderly maintenance man from the clinic. Her stomach tightened in fear for Joseph now as well as for herself. Any man sent to deliver this message would be ruthless and would have no qualms about killing Joseph. But, to Shelby's relief, the man who held her must not have perceived Joseph as a concern. He didn't even spare Joseph a glance. Message delivered, he released her. All of Shelby's weight had been balanced on him and she fell onto her hands and knees on the stained and broken asphalt. He stepped over her and strolled out of the alley.

"Lady! Lady! You all right?"

Joseph again. Shelby coughed and struggled to get up but couldn't manage to do so. Then Joseph was there in the alley with her. His face, worn and creased like old leather, bent to hers.

"It's you, Dr. Grant! Dr. Grant are you hurt?" Without waiting for a response, Joseph pulled a cell phone from the shirt pocket of his blue uniform. "I'm calling for an ambulance. You hold on, Dr. Grant."

* * *

Chief Of Police Mitchell Turner took the next turn, taking him onto the interstate leading out of Blake County, New York. Cars sped by his SUV making a soft whooshing sound. His police radio was tuned low though he could still make out the nasal voice of the woman working dispatch tonight.

Mitch cast another glance at his rearview. A late model sedan and a compact were still behind him where they'd been since he'd taken the on-ramp and pulled out in front of them. No other vehicles had followed him onto the highway.

Ten minutes later he was still in the clear and turned onto the deserted stretch of road that would take him to his destination. Trees lined both sides of what passed for this road and rose high into the sky but moonlight filtered through the branches, lighting his path. Gravel crunched beneath his tires, making a silent approach impossible if he'd wanted one. He didn't. He wanted the man he was meeting, Dan Harwick, to know he was on his way.

Harwick was working undercover, investigating Christopher Rossington whose business dealings were a front for organized crime. On the phone earlier today, Harwick sounded ... tense. A first for the cool-under-fire Harwick. Another first for Harwick was this request for an unscheduled meeting tonight. Mitch had never known Harwick to alter a plan and it concerned him.

Harwick had told Mitch he'd be driving a pickup truck for the meet. Mitch's headlights illuminated a truck parked at the edge of the road and Mitch was glad to see Harwick inside the vehicle. Harwick's cheeks hollowed as he drew deeply on a cigarette and the tip of the smoke glowed red. Mitch flicked the high beams as they'd agreed and pulled up alongside the truck.

Without preamble, Harwick said, "We got trouble, Mitch."

"Tell me."

Harwick met Mitch's gaze. "Rossington's got a mole in our investigation."

Mitch had taken care to keep a tight lid on the investigation, restricting access to information, keeping status strictly need-to-know but he didn't ask Harwick how he knew about the mole or doubt that it was true. If Harwick said it, it was fact. "What do you know?"

Harwick took another drag on the cigarette then crushed it against the doorframe with a lot more force than was necessary to extinguish it. "Nothing. No face. No name. All I know is that our mole exists."

Harwick's anger was palpable. Mitch could well relate. There were only a handful of people working the Rossington case, and Mitch had selected each one of them. The mole could only be someone he knew. He tamped down on his rage for the moment. First things first. "What about you? How's your cover?"

"Solid. They're bringing me in deeper every day. Local business man, my ass." Harwick sneered. "Fuck, Mitch, this guy is into everything dirty and depraved." Harwick's lips thinned. "I want to nail Rossington by his balls."

Yeah, Mitch wanted that badly. "We'll get him, Dan."

Harwick gave one swift nod.

"I'll be in touch," Mitch said.

"What are you going to do about the mole?"

A rush of anger heated Mitch's face. "I'm going to find that bastard."

* * *

A 911 call would bring the police. Shelby couldn't let that happen. She couldn't let the police find the messenger. If her association with the messenger and the man who sent him was discovered ... she couldn't let herself think about the consequences of that without losing her mind.

As she sucked air into her starved lungs, she scrambled for a reason to stop Joseph but fear had numbed her ability to think and before she could come up with an excuse, Joseph had made the call.

She had to get out of here before the police arrived. Again, she tried to gain her feet but her arms and legs felt as strong as overcooked noodles.

"Should you be movin' around, Dr. Grant? Better to stay put, I think," Joseph said. "You should stay put till the ambulance gets here."

"I don't need an ambulance." Her throat burned from the messenger's choke hold on her neck and her voice came out raspy, belying her statement.

Deep crevices cut into Joseph's brow and his eyes narrowed in concern behind wire-rim glasses. But when Shelby continued to struggle, Joseph grasped her arm.

"Here let me help you, Dr. Grant," Joseph said.

Joseph hovered at her side as she ignored pain in her middle where the messenger had squeezed her, and made her way from the alley and back to the street. Her purse and briefcase were in front of the clinic where she'd dropped them. Shelby bit back a moan of pain and bent to snatch up the items. She dug inside for her cell phone. Her hands were shaking so badly the phone slipped in her grasp. She let out a whimper of frustration and fear, then locked her fingers around the phone and sent a text message. One asterisk. The man who'd sent the messenger to her tonight had devised a single star as their signal to meet.

He had to meet with her tonight—now. She had to assuage the anger that had prompted him to send her this warning. She squeezed her eyes shut. She had to drive home the depth of her commitment to him. Though how he could doubt that, doubt her ...

Shelby opened her eyes and stared at the phone, willing to see an asterisk in response.

Praying to see one. Seconds ticked by and the screen remained dark.

Tick. Tock.

Fear filled her and a scream began to build. She bit her lip hard to suppress it, breaking the skin and tasting blood.

"Dr. Grant, you want to call someone?" Joseph said. "The Chief? You're shaking something awful and no wonder at all. Here, let me call Chief Turner for you."

Calling the man she was engaged to marry would be the normal thing to do, but Mitch was the last person she wanted to see now.

"No!" In her anxiety, in her panic, the word erupted from her before she could stop it. Joseph's frown deepened at her vehemence. She swallowed and tried to think, tried to sound sane. She pushed hair back from her face. The strands were damp with perspiration brought on by fear. "No need to call Mitch, Joseph. No need to worry him." She swallowed. "I just—just want to put this behind me and go home." Though his intervention had done her more harm than good, she couldn't discount that Joseph had put himself in harm's way for her. There hadn't been many people in her life who would do that. Ignoring her stinging palms, where bits of gravel had cut into them when she'd landed on the ground in the alley, she reached out and clasped Joseph's arthritic hand. "Thank you. Thank you for everything you did tonight."

Joseph ducked his head and mumbled something but she didn't catch the words. Her attention became riveted on an ambulance and the patrol car right behind it that turned onto the street.

Both vehicles screeched to a halt at the curb, sirens blaring, roof lights flashing. Neighborhood residents, no doubt alerted by the wailing sirens, poked their heads out their front doors. Some left the confines of their homes to stand on their lawns and peer across the street while others ventured nearer, taking up positions on the chipped sidewalk and the brown grass in front of the clinic.

A cop and a medic exited their respective vehicles and began closing the distance to Shelby. She didn't want a report of this incident. She needed to send both the medic and the cop on their way.

As the men reached her, and she was about to do just that, a black SUV she knew all too well pulled in behind the cop car. The driver's side door was flung open and before the SUV had rocked to a stop, Mitch charged out. Her stomach clenched then dropped.

Mitch was dark-haired and tall with a hard, tough body. Standing above those around him, his eyes, a deep penetrating blue, landed on her. He kept his gaze trained on her as he made his way through the men and women that blocked his path to her.

Shelby tilted her head back to continue to look at him as he stopped in front of her. "I thought you'd be home by now."

Was she going into shock? Of all the things to say to him, that had to be the most inane. Mitch must have thought so as well because his gaze on her intensified.

"Had a meeting," he said softly.

He still wore the charcoal-gray suit he'd had on when he'd left for the police station that morning, though the tie was no longer knotted and hung loose on his crisp white shirt. The jacket was open, showing his paddle holster and cell phone on either side of his belt.

His brows were low, his handsome face pulled taut with worry. He lifted a hand to her neck and his gaze hardened. It was obvious by his expression that the skin there was marked. So much for keeping what had happened today from him. Her struggle with the messenger had left marks on her that she would never have been able to hide from Mitch.

Despite the look in his eyes that was now lethal, Mitch wrapped his arms gently around her and drew her against his body. "Are you hurt anywhere else? Did he—"

She didn't need to clarify what he was asking. She shook her head quickly, hastening to reassure him, of this, at least, and ease his fear. "No."

Mitch's hold on her tightened. She ignored the pain in her middle made worse by his fierce grip and wound her arms around him. For just this moment, she gave in to her need for him. Allowed herself the delusion that she was safe. That she wasn't alone. That what she had with Mitch was real.

He held her for a long time. She let him hold her far longer than she should have, undermining her intention to show him that what happened tonight was not as significant as he believed it was. It was significant, all right. Just not for the reasons Mitch thought.

Finally, he pressed his lips to her brow. He drew back slightly, just enough that he could look at her. "Have you been examined, honey?"

"Just got here myself, sir," the medic said.

Mitch rubbed his hands up and down her arms, left bare by the sleeveless pale blue dress she wore. Goose bumps had pebbled her skin. He removed his suit jacket and placed it around her. When he tried to pry her cell phone from her cold fingers, Shelby held tighter. If Mitch wondered about her strange attachment to the phone, he didn't press the issue and let her continue to hold it. With one arm around her, he gently led her to the ambulance.

There was no point denying the medic now. Any hope she'd had of keeping the attack from Mitch was long gone. She'd only draw more attention from him if she didn't allow the medic to examine her neck and to treat her abraded palms. After, she declined riding on to the hospital for a more thorough examination.

Mitch didn't look pleased with that. "Honey, you should be seen by a doctor."

Shelby shook her head. "That's not necessary."

At her hoarse voice, his eyes narrowed. He looked about to make a stronger case for a hospital visit then released a breath and let the matter drop. He received instructions from the medic on what to watch for that would suggest a complication from the trauma she'd sustained to her neck, then led her to his vehicle. He positioned her with her side against the passenger seat and with her feet on the running board. Leaving the door open, he stood in front of her. He ran his thumb along her cheek. "What happened tonight?"

Shelby closed her eyes.

"Take your time."

He thought she needed time to fight back the trauma of being attacked before she could respond. While that would certainly be believable, what she needed time for was to decide what to tell him. How much to tell him. His touch was gentle, so tender, tears welled in her eyes.

Mitch brought her close again. "Easy, baby. Take it slow."

Her hands were against his chest, her fingers curled around his shirt. She forced herself to release him and brought her hands together in a tight grip. "There isn't much to tell." She cleared her raw throat carefully. "I was leaving the clinic and a man came up behind me."

Mitch's body tensed though his arms around her remained gentle. "Take me through it."

His tone was calm but his eyes were fierce. His gaze remained on hers and fearing that her own gaze was too open just now, she lowered it to her hands. She gave him an edited accounting of the incident, leaving out that the man had spoken to her and what he'd said. She didn't want to mention Joseph but couldn't see a way out of that. Mitch was sure to find out about Joseph and would consider the man a witness. Fear of what Joseph may have seen made the fine hairs on the back of her neck rise. "Jo-seph called out," she went on, "and the man who held me released me and ran a-way. I was in the wrong place at the wrong time." She needed Mitch to believe that.

He didn't respond to that but asked instead, "Did you get a look at him?"

"Too dark and he was behind me the entire time." That, at least, was the truth.

Mitch rubbed her shoulder. "Okay. Don't worry about that. There are other ways to find this bastard."

Shelby's throat tightened. "I just want it to be over."

She didn't want Mitch pursuing this but how to deter him? Any logical woman—logical person—would want a violent man off the streets for their own peace of mind as well as to prevent him from hurting anyone else. Added to that, she was a psychologist who counseled survivors of violence. She saw up close how violence devastated lives and had dedicated her career to helping her patients overcome such trauma so they could resume their lives. Dealing with violence—living with violence—weren't foreign to her. She'd known all about the shattering effects of violence long before she'd met any of her patients.

"Chief? Dr. Grant?" Joseph said.

Joseph and Mitch were acquainted from times Mitch had stopped by the clinic to see Shelby.

Mitch kept one arm around Shelby as he turned to greet Joseph. Mitch held out his hand. "Mr. Bowden. Thank you."

Joseph shook Mitch's hand. "I didn't do anything, Chief. I'm just glad I picked that moment to take out the trash." Joseph shifted position, shuffling his feet in his brown polished shoes. "I overheard you sayin', Dr. Grant, that you were in the wrong place at the wrong time, like the attack was random. I'm not so sure about that."

CHAPTER TWO

At Joseph's words, Shelby's blood felt as if it turned to ice. Could Joseph have possibly overheard what the man said to her in the alley?

Mitch turned to Joseph now, giving the other man his full attention. "Why do you say that, Mr. Bowden?"

Joseph rubbed his nape where a strawberry birth mark colored the skin beneath his hair line. "Beggin' your pardon, Dr. Grant, but what you do here, helping these hurt ladies with your talk, and getting them and their children into shelters where they can be safe from their men who hurt them, well, that might not go over so good with their men."

Mitch's gaze sharpened. "Anyone in particular you think might want to hurt Shelby?"

Joseph cast a glance at Shelby then shook his head. "Just sayin'."

"You can be sure we'll look into that, Mr. Bowden," Mitch said. "I'd like to get a statement from you about what you saw tonight."

"Sure thing, Chief."

Shelby's breathing quickened at that.

Mitch called out to the young officer who'd arrived with the ambulance—Officer Worth, Shelby learned—and arranged for Worth to escort Joseph to the police station.

When they were alone, Mitch turned to Shelby again. "I need a few minutes here, then we'll head over to the station as well. You going to be okay?"

Shelby nodded.

Mitch held onto her a moment more, then left her to speak with the officers who'd arrived at the scene. A short while later, a canvas of the people milling about and of the neighborhood was underway and officers, armed with flashlights, entered the alley.

Shelby was still clutching her cell phone. There'd been no response from the man she so desperately needed to hear from. She had no choice but to wait on his whim to respond. The power was all on his side. He controlled when they met. Just as he'd controlled everything in her life for the last six months. She closed her eyes against the horror of what her life had become.

"Shelby?"

Mitch's urgent voice startled her and her eyes flew open. He reached out and framed her face between his large hands. The worry in his eyes showed her what a poor job she was doing of playing this down. Where was the strong woman of the last six months? *Somewhere back in that alley.* She fought back the thought. She had to pull herself together.

She lifted a hand to one of Mitch's and curled her fingers around his. "I'm okay, really."

He leaned in and pressed a kiss to her forehead. Tears stung and she squeezed her eyes to hold them back. At the start of all this, she hadn't expected to ever have Mitch's love and support. She couldn't have known how much having them would come to mean to her.

Mitch released her and she swung her legs into the vehicle. He closed her door then took his place behind the steering wheel. The drive to the police station passed in silence with Mitch trading glances between her and the street.

The station was quiet. A detective sat at his desk, two-finger typing. The smell of stale coffee hung in the air. Worth had arrived just ahead of herself and Mitch and had taken Joseph to an unoccupied desk in a corner of the room. Mitch had her hand firmly in his and led her to where Joseph and his officer were seated.

Mitch stopped in front of Joseph. "Mr. Bowden, I'd appreciate if you'd wait here while Officer Worth and I speak with Shelby alone now."

Joseph nodded. "Take your time, Chief."

Mitch's office was dark behind the large glass window. He flicked on lights and the harsh fluorescent overhead showed his desk that he kept neat and with a minimum of accessories. A bookcase backed against one wall.

Worth closed the door behind himself then took up a position there, notebook in hand, to take down what she told them, no doubt. Shelby tensed in anticipation of adding one more lie onto the pile she'd told in the last months.

Mitch held a cloth covered chair for Shelby. She was moving stiffly since her encounter with the messenger. She tried to hide it from him, to downplay the incident, but he frowned and she saw that she'd failed.

His grip on her chair lingered, then he released the scratchy synthetic and went to stand in front of her, leaning back against his desk. "Joseph Bowden seemed very concerned that your attack may have stemmed from your work at the free clinic. Have any of your patients' husbands threatened you?"

Shelby joined her hands in her lap. "No."

"Have any of these men approached you?"

"No."

"Any new patients? Did you end a personal or professional relationship recently?"

She gave him a shake of her head.

"Have you met any new people lately?"

"No."

"I need you to make a list of your friends, colleagues, and acquaintances. Don't leave anyone out, no matter how removed you think they may be."

She spread her hands then clasped them again. "You know the people I know."

His voice went soft. "I don't want to overlook anything, honey. We need to find out who you've been in contact with. If someone in your life wants to hurt you. Tell me again what happened when you left the clinic."

She did then added in a whisper, "That's all of it, Mitch."

"Okay." He took one of her hands, that had gone numb from her tight grip, in his own. "After I speak with Joseph Bowden, we'll go home."

* * *

Worth left to get Bowden. Shelby followed him out. Mitch watched her leave. She was only going to the outer office, but he didn't want to let her out of his sight, out of his arms. When he'd been notified about the 911 call from Bowden, fear and rage had surged through him. While his initial fear for her well-being had been laid to rest, he hadn't cooled off. The thought of someone hurting her made him want to hurt that someone.

Joseph Bowden stuck his head into the office. "Chief? Officer Worth said you want to talk to me now?"

Mitch put that thought on hold and brought himself back to the moment. "Come in, Mr. Bowden."

Joseph was in his late seventies. He was a retired school caretaker who still wanted to contribute. Shelby had told Mitch she'd learned of Joseph through one of her patients at the clinic where she volunteered Thursday evenings. The clinic had been in need of a maintenance man and after meeting with him she'd recommended Joseph for the position. In his few encounters with Joseph, Mitch had found the man to be devoid of bullshit, a trait Mitch found refreshing.

Mitch gestured to one of the chairs in front of his desk. "Have a seat, Mr. Bowden."

Joseph nodded but didn't sit back on the chair, rather perched on the end of it. His shoulders stooped on his thin frame. Worth returned and resumed his stance against one wall.

Mitch went around his desk and lowered himself onto his own chair. "I'd like you to take me through what you saw earlier tonight."

Again, Joseph nodded. He smoothed back the few remaining strands of white hair on his head. "I went out back of the clinic into the alley to take out the trash and dump it in the Dumpster there. I saw a woman being attacked in the alley."

"You didn't recognize Shelby?"

"No, sir. Not at first. Not then. There's no light in the alley. It was only the bit of moon out tonight that gave off enough light for me to make out a man and a woman. I didn't know the woman was Dr. Grant until I got to her. I never saw the man's face at all."

"How tall was the man?"

Joseph shook his head slowly.

"Taller than Shelby?"

Joseph nodded. "Oh, yes."

"Did Shelby's head block his face?"

"No. The top of her head was somewhere down around his shoulders." Joseph raised an index finger that was bent and misshapen. "Taller and wider, too. Looked to be wrapped around her."

The bastard was big. Again, Mitch felt rage at the man. "How did he hold himself? You saw him release Shelby. How did he move? Fast? With a limp?"

Joseph's eyes became fixed on a point in the

distance then he shook his head slowly. "He took his time leaving the alley. Didn't rush."

Odd that the guy wouldn't have made a run for it when he'd been spotted. "What did his footsteps sound like? Quiet, like athletic shoes or slapping against the asphalt like dress shoes?"

Joseph squinted in concentration. "I heard his footsteps so he wasn't quiet but to tell the truth once he let Dr. Grant go, I stopped paying him any mind. I was thinking about her. I should have paid him more attention so we could catch him." Joseph let out a little grunt of frustration.

"You're doing fine, Mr. Bowden. I'm going to have our artist speak with you. You may recall something more about the man's appearance."

"Sure thing. I'll do anything to help Dr. Grant. Chief, before, when I said what I said about maybe the guy who hurt Dr. Grant being one of the men of the women she helped?"

"What about that?"

Joseph rubbed the back of his neck. "I didn't want to scare Dr. Grant anymore than she was scared a'ready by saying this in her hearing, but I got something more I need to tell you about what happened to Dr. Grant tonight."

Mitch eyed Joseph. "What's that?"

"Earlier tonight, 'afore that man hurt Dr. Grant, I was in the hall, mopping the floors and that Sal Delrico showed up."

Mitch leaned forward. "Who is Delrico?"

"The man of one of the women Dr. Grant helped."

"Did he approach Shelby?"

Joseph shook his head. "No, sir. She wasn't

even at the clinic yet." Red suffused Joseph's skeletal cheeks. He jutted out his chin. "Delrico asked me where she was at and I wouldn't tell him nothin' except that he had no call to be botherin' Dr. Grant. He got powerful mad. Saying how it was her fault that his wife left him and took their kids. That he wanted to know where his wife was at. I told him he had to leave right then and there. He said he would go, but he'd be back."

Mitch felt rage he'd never known before. "You know where this Delrico lives?"

"I helped his wife, Louisa, home with some groceries one day when he'd hurt her too bad to take the bags home herself. Yeah, I remember where he lives." Joseph's lip curled as he recited the address.

Mitch turned to Worth. "Pick up Delrico." Mitch clenched his teeth with a force that made his jaw ache. "I want to talk to him."

Worth nodded and left Mitch's office.

"Dr. Grant is good people, Chief," Joseph said. His protuberant eyes glittered like marbles with his conviction. "We need to make sure we get this guy so he doesn't have a chance to go after Dr. Grant again."

Mitch nodded at Joseph's fierce loyalty to Shelby. "My thoughts exactly."

* * *

Mitch escorted Shelby from the station. The night air was cool as summer was losing its grasp to autumn. Despite his suit jacket atop her dress, she crossed her arms against the chill. Mitch put his arm around her, giving her his warmth.

Shelby had a town house from before they got together. A place she'd rented when she left her psychology practice in France, and returned to the U.S. six months earlier to settle in Blake County. Though she spent most nights at his place, she hadn't yet given up the lease. He'd asked her about that and received a vague response, just as she'd been vague about setting a wedding date. He didn't care for that thought or the niggling doubt that accompanied it. He blew out a breath. He had a more immediate concern: Shelby's safety. He didn't ask her where she wanted to spend tonight. He was taking her home with him.

He left the noise and congestion of the downtown core of Blake for the quiet suburb where he lived. The houses here were modest but well maintained. As he pulled into his driveway, the light he'd installed above the garage came on, illuminating the front of the house.

Shelby's attacker hadn't taken her key ring which held keys to his house as well, but Mitch wasn't taking any chances. He turned to her. "Wait here. Keep the doors locked."

At her nod, he left the vehicle. He removed his gun from his holster and did a sweep of the area around the house. When he deemed it clear, he went inside. All was clear inside as well.

He returned to his vehicle and took Shelby back to the house. Inside, he said, "Let's get you to bed."

Upstairs, Shelby entered the bathroom that

adjoined the master bedroom. She emerged twenty minutes later, fresh from the shower. Her soft brown hair was still damp despite the hair dryer he'd heard through the closed door. She was dressed for bed in one of his college football T-shirts that hung down to her knees. Mitch had switched on a lamp which showed the room decorated in shades of brown, and Shelby's face that was far too pale.

She joined him beneath the sheets of his king-sized bed. He opened his arms and when she went into them, brought her tight against him. The need to keep her close, to keep touching her to assure himself that she was all right hadn't eased. He saw the worst humanity could do to each other on a daily basis and was acutely aware of how much worse things in the alley could have gone down.

Her body remained stiff with stress and tension and she didn't sleep immediately. When she did, her rest was fitful. He hated that there wasn't a damn thing he could do about that.

He was still awake when a tremor rocked her body. A small cry followed it.

"Shelby?" Mitch rose onto an elbow and peered down at her. The moonlight streaming in through the slats in the blinds revealed that her face was now almost as white as her pillowcase. Tears leaked from her closed eyes. He thumbed them away. "Shelby." His throat tightened and his voice sounded as rough as gravel. "Wake up, honey." He removed his hand from her face and gently rubbed her shoulder. "You're dreaming."

Her breath was coming so fast she choked

before she managed to say, "Mitch?"

"Here, baby." He brought her flush against him. "Right here."

She pressed her face against his chest as if she could burrow inside him. Fury filled him. If he got his hands on the man who'd attacked her, he would surely kill him.

Shelby shifted in his arms. She lifted her head from his chest. "I'm keeping you awake."

"You can't think I care about that." He touched her face, caressing her cheek and then her lips. "I can't stand that you're too afraid to sleep because of that bastard tonight." Mitch clenched his jaw briefly. "You can go ahead and rest. You're safe, baby. I'm not going to let anyone hurt you." She made a small mewling sound and her eyes widened on him, filled with what he could only describe as desperation. His hand stilled on her cheek. Alarm tightened his gut. "What is it?" Her lips quivered. For an instant, he had the impression there was something she wanted to say to him, but just as quickly, her eyes cleared and the moment passed. Not so for him. He continued to see her frightened face in his mind. He kissed her brow gently, keeping his lips there as he repeated. "I'm not going to let anyone hurt you."

Shelby's arms wrapped around him with what felt like all the strength she was capable of. She held him like that for a long moment then leaned back. "We both have full schedules tomorrow." She swallowed. "We should get some sleep."

Mitch tucked a strand of hair behind her ear. "Why don't you reschedule your patients and stay home for the day?"

She shook her head. "Being at work will give me something else to focus on. If I'm here, all I'll be thinking about is what happened tonight. I need to go to work."

He had a need to protect her. To make sure nothing bad ever touched her again. He wanted her in a place where he could watch over her, but he could see the truth of her words in her eyes. This wasn't about his needs but about what was best for her and she appeared to be hanging on by a thread. "If that's what you want." And he'd make damn sure she was protected at work.

He encircled her in his arms and laid down with her once again. Eventually, her breathing grew deep and even. Mitch continued to stare into the darkness for a time before finally succumbing to sleep himself. He didn't think he'd slept long when he came awake with a start. Shelby was no longer in bed with him.

She wasn't in the bathroom. Telling himself he had no cause for alarm, she was home, she was safe, he made his way downstairs.

He found her in the kitchen. It wasn't surprising that she hadn't been able to turn it off for the entire night. He would have been surprised if she had been able to.

The kitchen was a blend of corals and beige made dim now with only the bulb over the stove providing light. Vertical blinds, in a deeper shade of beige, blocked out any moonlight. Shelby sat on one of the high wrought-iron stools at the breakfast bar, hunched over his laptop.

"Hey," he said softly as he entered the room.

She gasped and whirled around to face him.

"I'm sorry. I didn't mean to startle you."

She closed the lid of the laptop. "I was just getting started on that list you asked me for."

The list of names of her colleagues, friends and acquaintances, Mitch recalled. He wouldn't have thought that's what she'd been doing. Judging the haste with which she shut the laptop, he figured she was making notes on one of her patients that she didn't want him to accidentally see, though he did find it curious she would do so on his laptop when hers was on the dining table a few feet away. Likewise with her list.

The pulse in her neck was beating as fast as bird wings. He went to her and placed his hands on her shoulders. Her muscles were bunched tight. Gently, he kneaded the knots. His instinct was to try to take her mind off anything that upset her but maybe making the list wouldn't do that. Mitch's experience with survivors of violence extended only to gathering the facts about the nature of the crime. Maybe compiling the list would help to restore some of the control that son of a bitch tonight had ripped from her.

Added to that, he wanted that list. Sooner rather than later. In this instance, he had to stop thinking like the man who loved her and think like a cop.

Wound tight as she was, he didn't think she'd be able to go back to sleep in any case. "How about a cup of that tea you like so much?"

She nodded.

He filled the kettle and placed chamomile tea in a mug. While he waited for the water to boil, he filled the coffee maker for himself then took a seat beside Shelby. Her hands were clasped tightly on the counter. He brought one of them to his lips then said softly, "Let's get started on those names."

CHAPTER THREE

Shelby entered the building that housed the offices of the psychology practice where she worked, as well as offices for an accounting firm, a law firm, and an investment firm. Mitch was at her heels, his hard gaze missing nothing as he did a sweep of their surroundings. He'd insisted on driving her in to work and would be picking her up at the end of her day.

The building security guard was at his post in the lobby. Gus was the man on duty today. He was speaking on the telephone and gave a quick nod when Shelby and Mitch went by him on their way to the elevators.

The reception area on the twelfth floor where the psychology offices were was unoccupied. Darla, the administrative assistant, with her full-bodied laugh and always full jar of jelly beans for the patients, was not at her desk.

When Mitch had looked his fill of the entire floor, he led Shelby to her office and gave her a soft kiss. "I'll see you later."

As Mitch left her, Darla entered the office with a cheery "Good morning" that was cut off with a gasp. Shelby knew what had alarmed the other woman. The messenger had left her with a nasty bruise on her cheek in addition to the ones on her throat.

"My, God, Shelby! What happened!" Darla asked.

Shelby gave Darla the same story she'd told Mitch of what had happened to her last night.

Darla shook her head. "You should have taken the day off, though knowing you, I'd guess you'd go crazy at home."

Darla was right, though not for the reasons she suspected. There still hadn't been any response to her asterisk text. "Mitch said the same thing about staying home, but I need to be here."

The door opened, requiring Darla's attention. Shelby was glad of the distraction that put an end to further questions. Her first patient had arrived.

* * *

After Mitch dropped Shelby off at her office, and the patrol car he'd ordered to remain in front of the building arrived, he got a call that Salvatore Delrico was at the station. Wherever Delrico had been, Worth hadn't been able to find him all night. Detective Casey Sloane had finally tracked Delrico down that morning.

Now Mitch stood behind the observation glass watching the man in the interrogation room, Salvatore Delrico.

Delrico fit Joseph Bowden's physical description of Shelby's attacker. Tall and wide. And Delrico had an ax to grind with Shelby. He looked good for the attack. But even if he wasn't the man in the alley last night, Delrico had gone looking for Shelby earlier that day. With what Mitch now knew of the man, Delrico hadn't gone in search of Shelby to chat about the weather. The thought of how that encounter was likely to have gone down with a brute like Delrico was enough for Mitch to want to take the man apart.

Mitch needed to reign it in, he knew that, but knowing that wasn't helping when every instinct in him was raging to make sure Delrico was not able to be near Shelby again.

"Sloane?" Mitch said to the burly red-headed detective standing beside him. "You're in the interview room with me."

Sloane pushed off the wall. "You got it, Chief."

Having Sloane present was going to be Mitch's one concession to Delrico so Mitch didn't end up killing him.

Sloane held up a folder labeled with Delrico's name. Judging the thickness, Delrico had been busy. Mitch glanced at the pages inside then handed the folder back to Sloane and pushed the door to the interview room hard. It hit the wall with a thud that reverberated in the room.

Mitch gave Delrico a full-on glare and held it. The other man had been sitting erect but now lost his cocky pose. He swallowed hard and his skin lost some of its healthy pigment.

"I'm Chief Turner," Mitch said. "Where were you yesterday evening between eight and nine?"

"At a friend's place."

"What were you doing there?"

"What's this about?"

Mitch gave the man a hard look. "Answer the question."

Delrico shifted on the chair. "My place is being fumigated. Needed another place to be."

"What did you do at your friend's?"

"Watched the tube."

"What was on?"

Delrico regained his arrogance and flashed a bright smile. "Had a DVD in the player. My friend has a copy of 'It's A Wonderful Life'."

Mitch wanted to punch that smile from Delrico's face, but held himself in check. Barely. "This friend there with you?"

Delrico smirked. "Nah. He's out of town on business. I was all by my lonesome."

"When was the last time you went to the Mason Street Clinic?"

Delrico's upper lip curled. "Don't remember."

"How about yesterday? Do you remember going there yesterday?" Mitch held Delrico's gaze and sweat beaded on the other man's brow.

"So what if I was there yesterday? It's a free country last time I checked."

"What did you do at the clinic?"

"I didn't do nothin', man."

"Why did you go there?"

"Not. Your. Biz."

Mitch sneered. "That so? Now you've made me curious, Delrico. I'm wondering what you did at the clinic that you can't talk about."

"Didn't say I can't. Said I won't."

Mitch goaded him. "Either way. A man who has nothing to hide wouldn't be afraid to answer a simple question."

"I ain't afraid of nothing! Got that!"

"Then you're even stupider than you look."

Delrico sprang to his feet and the chair he'd been sitting on hit the floor.

Bring it on. Give me a reason. Mitch would have liked nothing better in that moment than the excuse to pound on Delrico, but the man went still and a few seconds later righted the chair and resumed his seat. Evidently Delrico wasn't as stupid as Mitch hoped.

"Since you're going to find out anyway, if you haven't already," Delrico said. "I went to talk to Grant at the clinic."

"What about?"

"Don't play me, cop. I'm getting what this is about. That shrink behind this? She call you?"

"Why would she do that?"

"Because she's out to pin something on me. She's got my wife scared of me. Hiding from me. Maybe Grant has the hots for my wife and wants my Louisa for herself."

Mitch ignored the comment. "Dr. Grant doesn't need to pin anything on you, Delrico. I've read your arrest sheet."

"That's a lie. That Grant has brainwashed my Louisa into saying I hurt her. This is all that bitch Grant's doing."

Mitch got in Delrico's face. Teeth clenched, he said, "You'd do well not to refer to Dr. Grant that way in my presence."

Delrico jerked back. His eyes bulged with fear.

His Adam's apple bobbed several times before he said, "I love my wife."

Mitch remained in Delrico's personal space for another moment before straightening away from the man. He retrieved a photo from the folder Sloane held, then tossed it onto the table. It was Louisa Delrico after her most recent visit to the Blake Hospital. Louisa's face was swollen and so bruised she was barely recognizable. Her list of injuries included fractured ribs, broken bones and stab wounds. She'd required life support for a period of time.

"Yeah, I can see how much you love your wife," Mitch said. "If you loved her anymore that night, she'd be in the ground."

Delrico's face went beet red. He tensed, but this time remained in his seat.

"Good move," Mitch said softly, flattening his palms on the table top and, again, leaning in close to the other man. "I'm itching for a reason to lay you out. Now, what happened at the clinic?"

"Nothin'. Grant wasn't there. I talked to the janitor and then I left."

"But you went back."

Delrico shook his head. "If that's what Grant is telling you, then she's lying. I didn't go back there."

Despite his desire that Delrico was not being truthful and he'd found the man who attacked Shelby, Mitch's gut was telling him differently. That Delrico was telling the truth.

Needing to be certain, though, Mitch kept at the man, taking him back to earlier that evening asking how he'd spent his day then circling back to the hours between eight and nine p.m.

Though Delrico was looking tired and becoming irritable, his answers remained consistent. Mitch did not want to believe him which meant Shelby's attacker was still at large. At this point, however, he had no choice but to consider the possibility. Delrico was the scum of the earth and certainly capable of hurting a woman which he'd proved, but it did not appear that he was responsible for what had happened to Shelby last night. Still, Mitch wasn't ready to abandon Delrico as a suspect.

Mitch left the interrogation room with Sloane in tow. In the hall, he turned to Sloane. "Delrico's alibi for the time Shelby was attacked is shaky. I want you to get on that. See if anyone in the building might have seen him. Heard him moving around inside this friend's apartment." Mitch paused, then added. "Cut him loose. Drive him home then watch him. I want him monitored overnight. I want to know if he goes out or if anyone comes to see him. Tell your relief to call me if there's any movement. I don't care about the time."

With his doubts about Delrico, Mitch needed to widen the net. Shelby had given him the list of names he'd asked for. Back in his office, he entered those names into the database. He was looking for anyone who'd had run-ins with the law, no matter how minor. The people in Shelby's circle of friends and acquaintances were not of the criminal variety, however, and no one hit.

Mitch drummed his knuckles on his desk.

Shelby wanted to believe her attack was random, but Mitch couldn't be sure of that. He had to consider that her attacker had chosen her. In his experience, people were not targeted without motivation. If someone had Shelby in his sights, he had a reason for targeting her. If Mitch dug into her life deeply enough, he'd find that reason.

And, not only her life, but his as well. He couldn't discount the possibility that someone with a grudge against him could have attacked Shelby as a way to get back at him.

Mitch rubbed a hand down his face. His mother had died of cancer when he was a boy. His dad was still living and local. His dad and Ellen, the nurse Ed Turner had fallen in love with and married, while recovering from a gun shot that had ended his career with the Blake County PD. There was also Mitch's brother who lived out of town with his family. Mitch would give them all a call, letting them know what was going on here and to be on the alert. But if Shelby's attacker was someone with a grudge against him then that person had made it clear tonight that he wasn't after Mitch's father or brother. No, if this bastard had looked into Mitch's life, he would know that Shelby was everything to him.

Yeah, he'd be looking at people with something against him. Mitch glanced at his watch. Shelby had been in her office for about two hours now. He had a cop parked outside the building. The building employed its own security in the lobby. Shelby was safe. Still, he picked up the phone and called her. Darla answered his call.

"Darla, it's Mitch."

"Hey, Mitch."

"Everything okay over there?"

"All's well. Did you want to speak with Shelby? She's with a patient and you know how she doesn't want to be disturbed when she's in session. If it's important, I could make an exception. Be aware that I'm taking my life in my hands if I interrupt her without cause." Darla laughed loudly.

"No, that's okay." Darla had given him the answer he needed. Shelby was all right.

"Any message, Chief?"

"No, thanks."

Mitch ended the call as one of his detectives stuck her head in his office.

"Chief, just wanted to let you know I'm here and the ADA just got off the elevator."

Mitch recalled the Assistant District Attorney was here to speak with him and the detective about a case coming to trial the following week. "Okay. Let's get started."

* * *

The rest of the day passed quickly as Shelby met with patients back to back and returned phone calls. Word of what had happened at the clinic spread quickly and she'd received several calls from her friends. She shook her head. Mitch's friends. The people she now called friends had all been Mitch's friends, initially. In the few short months, the people in Mitch's life had embraced her as if she'd always been one of them. Their easy acceptance and concern meant more to her than they could ever know. Her family life had certainly never provided either. No, there'd been no loving home life for her. Her upbringing had been the stuff of nightmares. She pressed her lips tightly together, angry that those memories still had the power to hurt her. That she still let them.

Worse, it wasn't just memories. Her present remained horrific. She was ever stuck in the life she'd been born to, a vicious, endless cycle she was unable to break.

She stared at the phone. She'd heard from almost all of the people she knew except the one person she needed to hear from. There'd been no asterisk in response.

As if she'd willed it, Shelby's cell phone rang. Her heart sped up, but, no, no asterisk. Caller ID read Louisa Delrico. Though this wasn't the call she was praying for, Shelby's heart continued to race. She'd given Louisa her cell phone number with the hope that she would call for help to leave her husband. Louisa had done that and was now safe in a women's shelter. Had something happened? Shelby snatched up the phone. "Louisa?"

"Dottore di Grant."

Louisa sounded near tears. Shelby's alarm ratcheted up and her grip on the phone tightened. "Louisa, what's wrong?"

"I do not call about me. I read in newspaper that a man hurt you outside free clinic. You are okay?"

Shelby exhaled a long, slow breath. "I'm just fine. Thank you. How are you? How are you settling in there?"

"Everything here it is so nice. The other women, they are so kind. The newspaper, it did not say who was the man who hurt you. Was it Salvatore?"

"No." Shelby hurried to assure Louisa. "I think he knows that would only bring him more trouble. He's not going to find out where you are from me."

"Grazie, Dottore. Grazie mille. I am so afraid that Salvatore will hurt you for helping me."

"I'm fine, Louisa, really. Please don't worry about me. You just focus on getting better. When you're up to it, the shelter will help you relocate. Salvatore is out of your life forever. You and your children are safe and you're going to stay that way."

Louisa began to cry softly. "I do not know how will I ever thank you."

"Just get well. That's all I want."

"Si." Louisa stopped speaking for a moment then cleared her throat. "I go now, Dottore di Grant. Another woman, she wants to use the phone. Dio vi benedica. God bless you."

"Thank you, Louisa. Be well."

Louisa ended the call. Shelby held onto the phone another moment then slowly replaced it on her desk. Louisa was one more woman who'd escaped the abuse. One more woman who'd gotten herself and her children out. Not everyone got out ...

Shelby closed her eyes against a sudden onrush of tears.

Darla rapped gently on the open door and

stuck her head into the office. "I'm calling it a day, Shelby, if you don't need anything more?"

Shelby blinked quickly, clearing the moisture from her eyes, before meeting Darla's gaze. "No, go ahead."

Darla hesitated in the doorway, shifted her feet and her dark eyes narrowed. A worry line appeared on her forehead. "You're not going to be working late tonight, are you? I don't like the idea of you leaving here alone after dark."

Shelby shook her head. "Mitch is coming to get me. I'm a couple of steps behind you, I promise."

"I'll wait for Mitch with you."

"Really, go. Mitch will be here any minute."

"I'll stay." Darla pointed a finger at Shelby. "No argument." Before Shelby could respond, Darla glanced back over her shoulder. "Keith, what are you doing here? I thought you said you wouldn't be in until Monday."

Dr. Keith Ward along with Dr. Robert Sanderson were partners in the psychology practice. Shelby was an associate.

"Just need to pick up a file," Keith said.

"I'm heading home as soon as Shelby leaves," Darla said. "Do you need me for anything, Keith?"

"Nah. Go on. I can get my own files for once. I'll just have a quick word with Shelby before you ladies head out." As Darla backed out of Shelby's door, Keith entered her office. "Hey, Shelby." He jerked back. "Whoa! What does the other guy look like?"

It was a tactless remark, typical of Keith. She'd

often thought Keith had chosen the wrong profession. Shelby pressed her lips together briefly then said, "Not a scratch on him, I'm betting."

Keith dropped onto one of the maroon leather chairs across from Shelby's desk and linked his manicured fingers over the slight paunch that bulged beneath a designer shirt. "Shelby, got to tell you, you look like you went a few rounds with a heavy weight. Who'd you piss off? Surely not our police chief?"

"You really can be an ass, Keith." Shelby gave him a scathing look along with the same version of events that she'd given Darla and others all day.

"Damn." Keith shuddered. "Well, you'll be safe enough at night. Sleeping with a cop has its advantages."

Shelby didn't respond, but turned her attention to the papers on her desk, hoping Keith would take the hint and leave. No such luck, she realized, when he remained in the chair.

"I was going to mention this next week after Rob makes his announcement," Keith said, "but since we're both here now, I can't see any harm in spilling the beans. Just keep this on the Q.T. Rob plans to retire and sell his share of the practice. Before I start a list of candidates to take his place, I'm offering you his partnership. What do you say?"

For an instant, Shelby felt a thrill at the prospect. She enjoyed her work here. Did good work here. She thought of Louisa Delrico at the free clinic and others she treated here at her regular practice. In her professional capacity, she served a purpose. The only place in her life where she did. She would have liked to accept, but, of course, she couldn't. Her life was no longer her own. Had never really been her own.

She closed her eyes for an instant at that hard truth, then focused on Keith again. "I appreciate the offer, but I—"

"Don't say no so fast." He held up a hand. "Our patients love you and are recommending you all over the place which brings in more dough for us. Darla's as protective as a lioness where you're concerned. I know you like it here. Hell, we're irresistible." He waggled his thick brows. "It's win-win."

Shelby couldn't get into the spirit of Keith's humor. He was right about how she felt about her work and the people here. Hadn't she just been thinking the same?

"Don't say no right away. Take some time to think about it," Keith said.

Mitch knocked once sharply on her door.

"Hey, Chief," Keith said.

"Doctor."

"Glad you're here."

"Oh? Why is that?"

"I just made Shelby an offer I was hoping she couldn't refuse." Keith chuckled. "As it turns out, I think she can. I need reinforcements."

Mitch narrowed his eyes. "What was the offer?"

"A partnership in the practice." Keith got to his feet. "Do what you can to convince her, will you?"

Mitch offered no assurance that he would. Shelby knew he didn't like Keith. Keith would have no ally in Mitch.

Keith rapped his knuckles three times on Shelby's desk and gave her a wink. "See you Monday."

As Keith left her office, Mitch braced one palm on her desk and leaned toward her. With his other hand, he cradled her nape and drew out a kiss. Soft. Light. A gentle glancing of his mouth against hers. He slid his tongue over her lips, one at a time, then eased between them into her mouth. Shelby curled her fingers around the lapels of his suit jacket, feeling the hard muscles of his chest. As always when he touched her, her body responded to him. Desire had her juices flowing but what she felt for Mitch went beyond lust and her heart pounded with all the love she had for him.

Since the alley, he hadn't truly kissed her. He'd brushed his lips across her brow, and her hair, and touched his lips lightly to hers, but he hadn't kissed her with the intimacy of a man who knew every inch of her body and knew it better than she did herself.

He was being careful with her. Not wanting to do anything that would cause her more harm. It weighed heavily on her. Her story about the alley was just one more lie between them but right now it felt like one too many.

Mitch must have felt the change in her. He drew away but left his hand where it was, tenderly stroking the back of her neck. "Ready?"

His blue eyes had deepened. Desire burned in

his eyes now and love that burned just as hot. Seeing it and knowing it was all based on a lie brought Shelby near tears. She swiveled her chair away from Mitch on the pretext of filing a chart. She took her time with it and only when she'd regained her composure did she turn back to him. "All set."

Darla left the office with them and got into her sports coupe. Shelby followed Mitch to his vehicle and a few moments later they were in his SUV, driving back to his house. Traffic was heavy and came to a stop. Mitch's window was down and the odor of exhaust fumes and tar from a road repair drifted into the vehicle.

He turned to her. "A partnership offer? I'd say congratulations, but if it's something you have to be talked into, then it's not something you're interested in."

Shelby told Mitch of Robert Sanderson's imminent retirement that had prompted the offer. "I'm not sure I'm ready for long term there." She lied. "I'd like to keep my options open."

"You know best. I suppose you can stay on in your present position if you want to. If not, I'm sure you won't have a problem practicing elsewhere."

Her next place of employment would be very far from Blake County. Far from Mitch. Mitch's cell phone rang. While he took the call, she looked out her window to the stalled traffic, now cast in shadow by the setting sun, so he wouldn't see on her face the bleak turn her thoughts had taken.

"I called Gage, Ryan, and Zach and canceled the weekend."

Shelby went still then looked to Mitch. His call had ended and he clipped the phone back onto his belt.

"No." She heard panic in her tone and worked to quell it. "What I mean is it's not necessary."

His brows drew together. "There'll be other weekends, honey."

"We've all been looking forward to this."

"I just want you to take it easy for the next few days, baby." His voice was gentle. "Let me take care of you."

Shelby swallowed a knot in her throat. "I don't want what happened to change anything. I want to be normal. And you're not the only one looking forward to seeing our friends."

Mitch continued to study her. A silence ensued then he said, "You sure?"

"It's what I want, Mitch. I don't want to be thinking about this all weekend."

Traffic began to move again and Mitch resumed the drive home. He reached out across the console and took her hand in his, his much larger hand enveloping hers. "Why don't you give it some more thought. I can always call them back later tonight."

"I don't need to think about this," Shelby said. "It's what I want. Please let's just go ahead as planned."

CHAPTER FOUR

Mitch reached into the cooler at his feet for another beer. He was on his porch with friends, Zach Corrigan, Gage Broderick, and Ryan Crosby, who were visiting for the weekend. The front door was open to the screen. The mild day had remained so into the evening. A soft breeze was blowing, carrying the lingering scents from the grill where he'd cooked steaks and chicken a short while ago. Across the street, his neighbor's two young children splashed in a small inflatable pool.

The four of them were now lounging in lawn chairs, twisting the tops off bottles of beer and watching the sun go down. With Ryan heading up a division of the South Carolina PD and Gage still working for the Washington PD, spending leisurely days just hanging out could no longer be spontaneous but needed to be planned. Though Zach was local, he was in and out of the country on covert missions for the security firm he owned and operated with other ex SEALs. This get together had been in the works for weeks.

Still, if Shelby hadn't insisted that the weekend go ahead, Mitch would have rescheduled. Was this what she needed? A houseful of people to keep her from focusing on the attack? So far he hadn't seen much evidence that it was working. They'd spent yesterday evening, after the drive home, preparing for their house guests. While Shelby had thrown herself into the preparations of accommodations and food, Mitch could see her thoughts were elsewhere. And last night, again, her sleep had been restless and plagued by nightmares.

His friends' ladies had come along for the weekend. Gage's fiancée, Mallory. Ryan's wife, Tina. Zach's lady of the moment, Candy. Mitch turned his head to listen, but couldn't hear conversation from inside where Shelby was with the other women.

"Understandable that she's feeling off."

Mitch had told his friends of Shelby's attack when he'd initially canceled the weekend. He turned away from the door and faced Zach who'd spoken. Either Zach knew him too well, or he was as transparent as glass today. Likely both.

"Yeah," Mitch said. "Every time I think of that guy with his hands on her I want to break something. Break him."

"Any leads on the bastard?" Ryan asked. He'd been slumped in the chair, the beer bottle dangling between his knees, left bare by khaki shorts. He straightened his posture now, and his gaze sharpened, clearly awaiting Mitch's answer.

"We thought we had one." Mitch's grip on his beer tightened. "Asshole husband of one of the women Shelby counsels at the free clinic. Guy has an alibi but it's shaky. We have a witness, but he wasn't able to make the ID and his description to the artist was a bust. I want it to be the husband." Mitch spoke through his teeth. "He looks good for this. Rap sheet from here to the next county. All for beating his wife. He's no stranger to violence against women."

Gage's eyes narrowed and his brows pulled taut, puckering the scar at his hairline from a bullet wound he'd sustained a few months earlier. He'd been injured while working the human trafficking case that had brought him and Mallory together. "I hear a 'but' coming."

Mitch looked to Gage. "My gut is telling me this isn't our guy."

Zach lowered the beer from his lips. The movement shifted the sleeve of the deep green T-shirt he wore, giving a glimpse of the tattoo on his upper arm. "Could be a good thing. Better if the attack was a crime of opportunity. Some fucker who happened upon Shelby instead of targeting her."

"Yeah." Mitch's gaze went to the front door again. "The last thing we want is for someone to be fixated with her but I can't rule that out. I'm going through my files. I have to consider that someone from my past may be trying to hurt Shelby to get to me."

"Or someone from your present," Gage said. "Any developments with the case against Rossington?"

"Nothing yet." Mitch's jaw tightened. "I wouldn't put it past that son of a bitch to try to get to me through Shelby. For the time being, I'll be sticking to Shelby like glue."

"Damn straight." Gage inclined his head in one brisk nod. "How'd that go over when you told her? I can't see her wanting you hovering."

Mitch eyed his friend. "No doubt you're right but she isn't stupid and the situation is what it is. She'll deal."

Zach held up a hand for Mitch to toss him another beer. Mitch complied.

"If you're tied up and need me to escort Shelby anywhere," Zach said as he opened the bottle, "I'll be around for the next couple of weeks."

Mitch found his first smile. "I don't think you'll be readily available with Candy to keep you company."

Zach laughed. "She's something, that's for sure. I plan to spend as much time being horizontal with her as possible before the next job starts."

"Do you know where you'll be going?" Ryan asked.

"Yeah."

They all knew better than to ask Zach for an exact location or for details of the mission. Among Zach's clients was Uncle Sam himself. Details of the covert Ops Zach and his firm carried out for the government were classified.

A brief silence descended. Zach broke it and broke into a grin. "One of us has to carry the torch for bachelorhood with all of you clowns in relationship bliss."

Ryan's mouth tightened at Zach's statement. Ryan and Tina had been going through a divorce until Tina broke news to Ryan that she was pregnant with his child. Mitch recalled the late night call from Ryan. After Ryan had told Mitch about the pregnancy, he'd gone on to say that they were giving their marriage another try for the sake of their baby.

"How are things with you and Tina?" Gage asked.

"Peachy," Ryan said. He took a long swallow from his own bottle of beer. "Any of you catch the game last night?"

* * *

Shelby took a sip of wine and gave another surreptitious glance at her cell phone where it sat on the coffee table in the living room. Nothing. The screen remained dark.

Another day spent waiting, hoping, praying to see that single star appear on her cell phone screen. Her stomach was so knotted she hadn't been able to eat and yet felt on the verge of throwing up. She didn't know what she'd do if he didn't contact her soon.

"So, how 'bout it, Shelby?"

Shelby blinked. "Sorry, Candy, what did you say?"

Candy, Zach's current lady, bounced up from the dove gray carpeting where she sat cross-legged. The living room was a combination of dusky blues and various shades of gray. While Shelby had been lost in her own thoughts, the sun had lowered, throwing the room into twilight. She reached out and lit the lamp on an end table.

"No problem." Candy turned in a small circle in the middle of the room. "I was just saying let's call the guys in and play charades."

Candy's smile widened showing what was likely every one of her lovely teeth. She was stunning in face and form with long dark hair that fell blade straight to the hem of her barely-there mini skirt. Bubbly. Perky. Fun. That was Candy. In the time Shelby had known Zach, she'd come to see that Candy was his usual choice of female company when he needed some R & R between jobs.

Tina made a face. Her brows rose high and were covered by her auburn bangs. "I'm not as light on my feet as I was a couple months ago, girls."

Before she could stop it, Shelby's gaze went to the slight bulge in Tina's abdomen that marked her early pregnancy. Shelby's eyes stung and she made her way to the window to blink away the moisture before the other women could notice. Not quick enough, though, she realized as the conversation veered to Tina's pregnancy and babies in general and Mallory left Tina and Candy to it and joined Shelby.

"How are you really?" Mallory asked.

Shelby turned away from the thick oak on Mitch's front lawn to face Mallory. "I'm fi—"

Mallory held up a hand. "Don't tell me you're fine. No sane woman would be after being attacked."

Mallory Burke was an agent with the FBI. Just a few short months ago, she'd almost died in the course of an investigation. If anyone would know the trauma of finding one's self helpless and at the whim of another, it was Mallory. "How are you?" Shelby asked.

Mallory bowed her head. Her dark hair curtained her face. She brought her hands together then unclasped them, then linked them again. Her short nails, covered in clear polish, dug into her skin, leaving crescent shapes. "I still have some bad moments. Nightmares." She shuddered. "When I do, Gage is there to talk me down from the ledge."

Mallory stopped speaking, clearly overcome. Before Shelby could offer comfort, Mallory lifted her head. She rolled her eyes in an effort to lighten the mood, Shelby thought, though she could see Mallory was still affected. "If you need to talk," Shelby said, "I'm just a phone call away."

Mallory squeezed Shelby's hand. "Same here."

Mallory couldn't possibly know how much Shelby wished she could take her up on her offer. Shelby felt a pang, thinking how that offer would be rescinded if the truth about her ever became known. All this, here with Mitch's friends, was an illusion, all based on a lie. All this with Mitch was a lie.

"Hey, you okay?" Mallory asked.

Shelby shook her head at Mallory's question. "Sorry. I zoned out." She swallowed. "Candy, you said charades. C'mon Tina it'll be fun. I'll call the men in."

* * *

Shelby was glad to see the day end. Being "on" for Mitch's friends, putting on a show for them and for Mitch had taken its toll. She would have taken Mitch up on his offer to cancel the weekend get together if she hadn't thought it would be easier for her to slip away if she needed to with a house full of people to occupy him rather than if it were just the two of them.

Mitch came up behind her where she stood at the bathroom sink. "You're so quiet." He slid his arms around her waist and met her gaze in the mirror. "What you went through." His brows drew together. "Have you thought of speaking with someone?"

"I'm a psychologist, Mitch. I know how to treat trauma."

"Someone else's trauma. Right now you're the survivor. Baby, it wouldn't hurt to talk with someone."

Mitch had no way of knowing the last thing she could do was tell anyone the truth behind the attack. "Physician heal thy self," she said and worked up a smile.

Mitch's expression didn't ease. "Yeah, but no reason you have to. I won't ask if you're all right. Obviously you aren't and understandable that it's going to take time. What I will ask is what can I do?"

The concern in his eyes, his tight grip on her and the deep emotion in his voice brought a lump to her throat. Mitch was a man to share the good and the bad, though he had no concept of just how bad her bad was. She turned in his arms and pressed against him. His arms came around her more securely and he drew her tight to him.

"You're already doing it," she said. "You're already doing it."

But she couldn't let him continue to worry over how she was coping with what had happened in the alley. He deserved better. Alleviating his concern, though, wasn't her only reason for what she was about to do, not her main reason. She hated that it wasn't, that it couldn't be.

She could not let him continue to hover. She needed him to back off. The only way he'd do that was if she showed him that she was recovering from the attack. That the attack hadn't left her scarred. That much was true. The attack itself wasn't what had scarred her.

Shelby rose on tiptoe. She looped her arms around his neck. Mitch was a tall man and even with this added height, their mouths were not even close to being on a level. She tugged him so he would lower his head to hers. When he did, he kissed her gently, his lips brushing softly against hers. She knew he'd continue to be careful with her and when he would have raised his mouth from hers, she clutched his neck. She ran her tongue along the seam of his lips and when he opened his mouth, inserted her tongue and deepened the kiss.

Mitch raised his head. His gaze fixed on her, the question in his eyes obvious, as was the desire. His eyes had darkened with it. Instead of acting on that desire, he held back, raised a hand to cradle one side of her face. "I love you."

Any thoughts she had that she'd need to pretend. Need to put on an act to be convincing vanished. How she loved this man.

Mitch clasped her waist and lifted her so they were now eye-to-eye. She held his gaze as he brought her lips to his. He kissed her gently then fused his mouth to hers.

Without interrupting the kiss, he took one hand from her waist and lifted her under the knees. Holding her against his chest, he carried her to the bed and carefully lowered her to the mattress.

He got onto the bed with her and rose onto an elbow. He slipped a finger beneath one of the thin straps of the tank top with matching bottoms she'd donned for bed and lowered it. He did the same with the other strap. The tank held at the swell of her breasts. Mitch kissed her just above the tank. The kiss was so tender, almost reverent and her heart felt like it stuttered.

Then he lowered the tank and lowered his mouth to her breasts.

The touch of his tongue, his teeth softly scraping her flesh felt like an electric jolt. Shelby sucked in a breath and flung her arms to her sides which gave him greater access. Mitch took full advantage, kissing, laving, sucking each breast in turn. Though his breaths were becoming rapid and his hands less steady with his own mounting desire, he was patient, unhurried, and her pleasure grew and grew.

She wanted to touch him as well and tugged at his T-shirt. He bunched the shirt in one fist then yanked it over his head and tossed it into a corner of the room. She tugged at the zipper on his jeans next. Mitch lifted himself a little higher off the bed and was out of the clothing that covered his lower body as quickly as he'd shed the top.

Shelby didn't hold herself back from reaching out to touch, at first skimming her fingers over him then, needing more contact, she flattened her palms on his warm, taut flesh. He was magnificent, hard muscled, broad shouldered, narrow hipped. His erection was as magnificent as the rest of him. She lowered her hand and wrapped her fingers around him. He closed his eyes and groaned.

When he opened his eyes again, they burned red-hot. He kissed and licked a trail down her breasts, her belly, her hips. He spread her legs and stroked her with the back of his finger. His gaze intensified. His nostrils flared and his Adam's apple bobbed hard. He lifted her and brought her to his mouth.

At the first touch of his tongue on her, Shelby came off the bed and gasped his name. He swirled his tongue around her, again and again and again. Shelby was shivering, quivering. He sucked her into his mouth, swirled, then sucked, swirled then sucked, repeating the pattern. She moved her head back and forth on the pillow, his name a mantra on her lips.

Mitch kept up the pleasure. Shelby could feel the pressure building. Her heart pounded. Her breaths came in gasps. She tensed then cried out with the strength of an orgasm that rocked her body.

She was still trembling from the aftershocks when Mitch rose above her and nudged her legs wider. Gently, he began to enter her. His face pulled taut. Sweat broke out on his brow and his jaw clenched as he gave her his first few inches.

Shelby's heart began to race again at the sensations as he slowly gave her more of himself and swelled within her. When he was fully inside her, she wrapped her legs around him, keeping him deep. Mitch was straining, his body trembling as he began to move within her. He withdrew then entered her again. He kissed her open-mouthed, hot and wet, his tongue thrusting between her lips. Shelby clung to him, her fingers digging into his thick biceps and moved with him. Mitch increased the pace. Harder. Faster. Shelby's breathing shallowed then caught and she threw her head back as another orgasm went through her with the force of a hurricane.

"Shelby."

He spoke her name in a voice that had gone hoarse and drove into her. His body tensed then shook with his own release.

Their mouths were still joined and Mitch moved his lips against hers in a tender kiss. Shelby kissed him with all the love she had for him.

Mitch gently withdrew from her and lay on his back, wrapping one arm around her and tucking her at his side.

"Okay?" he asked.

She nuzzled her face into his shoulder and smiled. "Very okay."

He laughed.

They hadn't closed the window blinds. Moonlight streamed across the bed, illuminating the fawn-brown bedspread they hadn't taken time to remove that was now bunched around and beneath them. The moon cast a small glow on their bodies that were slightly damp with perspiration.

Shelby's body began to cool and she shivered. Mitch eased away from her and drew the bedspread over them, then wrapped her in his arms until every part of her was touching him.

Her body warmed but she didn't move away from him. Being here with Mitch was temporary. She was never more aware of that than in this moment. She blinked back the tears that flooded her eyes and melded her body with his.

CHAPTER FIVE

The signal to meet came the next morning. Shelby's stomach tightened at the sight of that single star even as her knees buckled in relief and she sank down on the tile floor in the bathroom. He hadn't shut down communication with her completely—her worst fear.

Mitch had been adamant about her not going anywhere unescorted. What to tell him so she could slip away?

Mallory was dishing scrambled eggs onto a plate when Shelby entered the kitchen. The scents of maple syrup and strong coffee carried on the air. Gage kissed Mallory's cheek then said something to her Shelby didn't catch and Mallory's laugh rang out.

Shelby cleared her throat. "Morning."

Mitch's gaze honed on her, assessing her, she knew. She forced a smile.

"Eggs are hot and I made pancakes," Mallory said.

"I haven't been much of a hostess," Shelby said. "Thank you."

Mallory added another pancake to the stack. "All I did was make some food."

Shelby gestured to the platters of food on the gleaming counter. "Everything looks great, but I'm going to have to pass on breakfast."

Mitch gave her a wink. "Not hungry this morning?"

A reference to the wonderful night they'd shared. He was teasing her. He was a man who was at ease in his own skin and as a result was an easy man to be with. She'd never known men like that, like him. The men in her world were nothing like Mitch.

On another morning, she would have kept up the sexual banter, volleying back and forth with him until they were both laughing and then loving. Not this morning. All she wanted this morning was to be on her way. She had to force herself not to bolt and looked up at him. "I have an emergency. One of my patients is in crisis and needs to meet. I have to go." She was wound tight and hoped he would take her anxiety over her patient as the reason for her distress. She dug into her oversized purse for her car keys.

Mitch set down his coffee mug. "I'll drive you."

"No need. I'll be at the office and you don't want to leave our friends and miss any of these last few hours with them before they leave for home."

Mitch kept his gaze on Shelby as he said, "Gage you understand my leaving, I'm sure."

"Absolutely," Gage said.

Shelby didn't want to protest further and risk arousing Mitch's suspicions, so she nodded. She hugged Gage and Mallory in a quick good-bye and asked them to let Ryan and Tina know why she wouldn't be seeing them off, then she and Mitch were on their way.

Traffic was light on a Sunday morning and the drive to her office went by quickly. Mitch insisted on taking her into the office complex and then up to her office where he did a thorough check of the floor and washrooms.

"I'll wait for you," Mitch said.

"I don't know how long I'll be."

"Doesn't matter."

Panic that Shelby hoped would pass for exasperation sharpened her voice. "Mitch my patient won't react well to seeing the police chief here. Please go and let me do what I need to do to help my patient." When he still hesitated, she added, "Charlie, the security guard, is right downstairs. You saw him. He's a Doberman when it comes to letting anyone into the building without authorization." She smiled to lighten the moment. "He's been known to ask for dental records as proof of ID." She leaned in and kissed Mitch then snagged him by the front of the T-shirt he wore over jeans and gave him a little push. "Now. Go."

He held back and brushed a knuckle down her cheek, then turned and left her.

She watched Mitch get into the elevator. Watched the numbers descend to the lobby. Gave him a few moments more to speak with Charlie and then to pull his vehicle away from the building. Taking the stairs, she went down the twelve flights and left the building from the side exit. She'd planned on having her car, but now hailed a taxi and gave the cabbie the address to the Blake Amusement Park with the added request to hurry.

The warm day had brought out families, and mothers, fathers, and grandparents rushed to the line to buy admission tickets to the park and strolled the grounds, often propelled by laughing children.

Shelby bought her ticket and wove through a knot of pedestrians gathered at the entrance who appeared to be deciding where in the park to go first. She had no such dilemma. She knew where she was headed and setting a brisk pace, made her way to the monkey cages.

He was waiting there, nibbling kernels of popcorn. She would have laughed out loud at that. His cuisine didn't lend itself to what he considered pedantic tastes such as popcorn. No, he considered himself too refined for such common food as that. He would no sooner eat popcorn than dress in a neon green T-shirt and ball cap, yet here he was, dressed just like that. An incongruous picture to the man he normally presented himself to be. She wouldn't have known him if she wasn't looking for him which was exactly as he'd intended.

He knew she'd arrived at the cages before she reached him. It no longer surprised her that he did. Her first attempt to catch him unawares had failed miserably and brought back to mind her earlier fears that the man really did have eyes in the back of his head or was he all knowing? He'd always been that way when it came to her.

He didn't turn to face her, didn't acknowledge her at all, but when she walked by the monkeys and onto the beaten path that led into the trees, he followed.

* * *

It went against everything in him for Mitch to drive off and leave Shelby in her office. He'd parked a distance away to avoid being spotted by her patient, in a location that gave him a view of both the front and side entrance to the building. From where he was he could observe all comings and goings. The one he hadn't expected to see going was Shelby.

The taxi that held Shelby pulled to a stop at the Blake Amusement Park. Mitch double parked his SUV, blocking a van, then ran after her.

She had a good head start and if he called out to her, she wouldn't hear him. What was she thinking, leaving her office and coming here where she would be vulnerable to another attack? The most likely reason was that the situation with her patient had changed and Shelby had needed to meet her or him here rather than at her office. She should have called him to let him know. He would have arranged some kind of surreptitious surveillance. But she wouldn't. Shelby would not risk compromising her patient.

The crowd was thick. People were enjoying the bright sunny day. Mitch lost sight of Shelby for an instant in what looked like a tour group milling around one of the animal houses but then she broke through, breezing by the monkey cages. She continued on into the trees. Damn it what was she doing? That thought was burning a hole in his stomach. Was she really meeting a patient? Mitch felt a spurt of anger with her for being so careless with her safety. A man left the monkeys as Shelby went by and headed in the direction she was going. A couple of seconds later, it was clear that he was following her.

Her patient? The man didn't appear to be in a hurry. He didn't appear nervous. In fact, he looked like he fit in well with the patrons of the park. Too well? The burn in Mitch's stomach became a four-alarm fire.

He ran after Shelby's pursuer. He continued playing catch up as Shelby and the guy went deeper into the trees. Oh, yeah. No doubt about it now. The guy was definitely following her.

Shelby had a destination in mind. That was also obvious. Mitch's guess was some spot where she could have some privacy with her patient. Whether or not this guy following her was that patient was still to be determined. Just where was she headed? Mitch couldn't tell.

He was still wondering that when Shelby stopped in her tracks and faced her pursuer head on. She must have known the man was behind her the entire time because her face didn't show any surprise. The man closed the distance between them and Shelby remained in place, watching his approach.

Mitch relaxed a bit at that. She knew this guy.

As bizarre a meeting place as this was, it looked like this was just that—an arranged meeting.

Mitch didn't intend to intrude. He wouldn't go back out and leave her completely defenseless here, but he'd continue to keep his distance. He was about to step back further into the trees so he wouldn't overhear her conversation but then the man with Shelby removed his ball cap and sunglasses, rifling his fingers through his thick, blond hair.

Mitch went still. He knew that man. Christopher Rossington. And here was Rossington meeting Shelby ...

* * *

Shelby felt as if pieces of her were falling off bit by bit. Her breathing was rapid and shallow and her heart drummed in her ears, blocking out all other sound.

She had to get it together before she turned and faced Christopher. If he thought she was losing her edge, that she was not capable, he'd write her off as useless and all would be lost. She squeezed her eyes shut for an instant, then turned and faced him.

His ice-blue eyes met hers. Cold. Unfeeling. Reminding her that there would be no reasoning with this man. She would have begged if it would elicit his compassion. It would not. He had none. He had no mercy. If she failed him, retribution would be swift.

"What do you have for me?" Christopher asked.

She bit her lip to stem the trembling. "Mitch is very close-mouthed about his work. It's going to take more time."

"You've had ample."

His unemotional declaration chilled her. "Mitch is a cautious man. An intelligent one. If he weren't, we wouldn't be here today. You would have been able to obtain the information you're after without me. It takes time to build his trust."

"Obviously, you haven't been successful at accomplishing that."

Her every fear was realized in that statement. She had to prove her worth to him. Everything depended on him believing that she was still of value to him. Her breaths shortened. Perspiration matted her blouse to her. There had to be something ... Shelby extended her left hand where Mitch's bold, square-cut diamond sat on her ring finger. As she wanted, Christopher's gaze lowered to the engagement ring. Her hand shook. She dug deep to find the resources to still the trembling.

"Mitch's coming around to trusting me, Christopher," she said. "He wouldn't marry a woman he doesn't trust. I have no doubt that given more time I can get what you need."

Her engagement to Mitch had given Christopher pause. She held her breath.

His gaze lifted to hers again. Flat. Reptilian. "I'll expect to hear from you with results very soon."

She released the pent up breath, but there was something more. She couldn't let him go without asking about ... without knowing about ... her stomach roiled as she summoned the courage to ask him the question that gnawed at her day and night. "About—"

"About what?"

There was a challenge in Christopher's softly uttered words and a spark lit in his eyes, daring her to go on, and showing her he would relish punishing her if she did. Shelby's heart clenched then began thumping wildly. She needed to ask her question. Needed to have him answer. She felt as if she was losing her last grip on her sanity but she was terrified of what he would do if she spoke the words and held them back. In a breathy whisper she said instead, "You can count on me."

He nodded and Shelby watched without blinking as he made his way back the way he'd come.

* * *

Christopher Rossington and Shelby. Mitch staggered against a tree. He felt as if the earth had shifted beneath him. He couldn't get his head around it, but he had to, of course. It had been all he could do not to charge through the trees and take Rossington apart.

Shelby wasted no time lingering on the dead end path and left as well. Mitch maintained his position, concealed among the trees until she'd passed him, then he trailed her. She veered in a different direction and when she emerged, it was into the high traffic area of the midway.

A cacophony of sounds hit him with a deep base blend. High-pitched squeals. Mitch watched

Shelby enter the Ladies room and then from there, she exited the amusement park and got into the first of a string of cabs lined up in the parking lot beyond the entrance.

When the cab Shelby was in pulled away, Mitch got into one as well and told the driver to follow her. He wasn't surprised when the cab left her once again at her office building. Of course, she'd need to be there so he could pick her up after her "session" with her patient.

Mitch watched her swipe a card against a key pad and then enter the building's side entrance, handily avoiding entering through the front and seeing Charlie, the security watchman, who would be witness to the fact that she'd left.

"Meter's running, man," the cabbie said. "You want to look some more?"

"No. I'm done here."

He figured Shelby wasn't going to be meeting with anymore criminals today and, fuck it all, he wasn't ready to face her. His truck was back at the amusement park. As Shelby disappeared into the building, Mitch told the cabbie to take him back there.

* * *

Back at her office, Shelby veered off to the restroom. Once inside, she bent over the toilet and vomited. Again. Then again. She'd thought she'd emptied all her stomach had in it in the amusement park washroom following her meeting with Christopher, but apparently, there was still something left.

After, she leaned back against the door of the stall, unable to stand without that support. She felt wrung out. Weak. Shaky. She hadn't been in Christopher's presence long but the fear had depleted her.

A glance in the mirror above the row of sinks showed her face pale and clammy. Her eyes wide and haunted. If Mitch saw her like this, there'd be no way to hold him off from wanting to know what had caused her such distress.

Since the night in the alley, she was barely holding him off as it was. How much longer before he caught her? He'd almost done that at his computer while she'd been searching for something to give to Christopher. She had to do a better job of maintaining the façade she'd created but she was cracking under the constant strain of desperation and fear. *All the king's horses and all the king's men ...*

A hysterical laugh bubbled out of her and she clapped her hand over her mouth. She gripped the counter and bowed her head. *She had to do this.*

She took several deep breaths then slowly raised her head. She rinsed her mouth and splashed cold water on her face before returning to her office. Not enough time had passed to make her excuse to Mitch of a patient emergency believable. She needed to extend the time.

Two hours later, she called Mitch and thirty minutes after that, they were back at his house. Gage, Mallory, Ryan, and Tina had left for home with Zach having taken them to the airport. Why Mitch hadn't been along for that, Shelby couldn't say since Mitch would have had more than enough time to see his friends off while she was away. He was tense, angry, had been since he'd picked her up and she couldn't account for it. Wondered about it.

She didn't need to wonder long. As soon as they were clear of the front door, Mitch turned to her. "How long have you been working for Christopher Rossington?"

Perspiration coated her skin. *Mitch knew.*

Teeth gritted, he said, "Answer me."

Shelby scrambled for some way to deny this but fear had overtaken her mind, leaving it blank. "I—I—"

Mitch's eyes glittered. "I said, answer me."

"What are you talking about?"

His lips thinned. "Don't play games with me."

Shelby stumbled for what to tell him—how to deny what he so obviously knew. All was lost if she couldn't come up with a plausible lie. She went on the offensive. "I don't like this line of questioning, Mitch. I'm not one of your suspects."

Mitch's jaw clenched. His tone was low, deadly. "I was there. At the park. On the path."

The blood drained from her head.

He raised his brows and pinned her with a glare. "I saw you with Rossington. I'll ask you again, how long have you been working for him?"

His expression, his eyes had gone hard. Her heart stuttered but she hadn't spent the last six months—God, her whole life—becoming adept at lying to fail now when everything that mattered was on the line. She laced her fingers together in a grip so tight her hands went white. "Whatever you think you saw ..."

Mitch's eyes went as dark as she'd ever seen them. "How long, Shelby?"

Shelby closed her eyes against the anger in his. It was clear on his face there was no point in trying further to deceive him. "Six months." The words came out in a whisper.

"Six months? We met six months ago. Convenient timing." His tone was sarcastic and bitter.

She opened her eyes. "Mitch ..."

"Give me a second here. I'm just getting that I've been set up." Fury sparked in his eyes. "Obviously meeting me at that fund raiser wasn't a coincidence."

Shelby licked her now dry lips then bit the lower one. "No."

"He put you onto me." Mitch spoke the words through gritted teeth.

Shelby's mouth trembled. "He wanted me to relay information about your investigation to him. He wanted to know what you knew. If you had an inside source in his organization."

Mitch's eyes bore into her. "Too bad your best efforts in the sack weren't good enough to get anything out of me."

She flinched and had to clear the tears that rose hot and fast to clog her throat before she could respond. "No, you gave me nothing. I stopped expecting that you would, but I had to hold onto that hope."

She wouldn't have believed it was possible, but

Mitch's expression grew more fierce. "I can't believe you're standing here telling me that you've been hoping for some way to get that bastard off. Do you not know what he is? How he makes his living?"

"I know."

If he'd been looking for a way to somehow excuse her behavior, to exonerate her, those two words only damned her. Mitch recoiled at that as if she'd pushed him, or, as if she now repulsed him. That cut Shelby to the bone, hurting more than she reasoned it should, given she'd known from the outset of this that her time with Mitch was borrowed and never real. Never hers.

"And yet you want him to get away with all he's done and to be able to continue." Mitch's nostrils flared. "Just who the hell are you?"

The disgust on his face twisted what felt like a knife to her stomach. "Mitch, please, hear me out."

"Oh, I intend to hear you out." A muscle pulsed in his jaw. "Down at the station where you'll give me a formal statement and I'll charge you with obstruction. At least."

Her stomach knotted. Her breathing shallowed. She took a step forward but didn't reach out to him knowing she was no longer welcome. "Please, Mitch. Please. I can't do that. This has to stay between us. Christopher can't know that you've found out about me. He can't know that you're onto me. We need to go on as we have."

He snorted. "You can't be serious."

"In public. In private," her voice cracked, "you

don't need to pretend." Shelby was thinking fast. "Mitch, please." The words came out in a rush. "You can't let Christopher know that you've found me out. I'll do anything to keep that from happening."

CHAPTER SIX

You can't let Christopher know that you've found me out. I'll do anything to keep that from happening.

Mitch figured that was the first true thing she'd told him in six months. Of course she wouldn't want Rossington to learn that Mitch now knew about her.

She'd set him up. Fed him a line. Got inside his head. But then she was a shrink and head games were her specialty after all.

He'd been right about the mole being someone he knew. Shelby was the mole. *Shelby.* He felt a level of hurt he'd never known before warring with anger. That hurt would bring him to his knees if he let it. He focused on the anger and the fury felt like a powder keg ready to explode.

"I want to know everything about your involvement with Rossington," Mitch said, "starting with if you managed to find out anything on your own that you passed along to him."

"If I'd found out anything and told Christopher, my job for him would have been complete and I'd be long gone. Since you overheard my conversation with him at the amusement park, then you heard me tell him that I still hadn't gotten any information. Christopher has to go on thinking I still can get him what he wants to know. Please, Mitch."

"I can't believe you're saying this to me."

"He has my daughter!"

Mitch stared at her.

"He has my daughter." Her voice broke.

Shelby's fear appeared so real that despite Mitch's rage with her, it got to him. "What are you talking about?"

"Christopher abducted her six months ago so I would spy on you for him."

"You have a child?" Mitch shook his head, taking that in.

"Sara." Shelby's voice quavered. "She's three years old."

"Why you?" Mitch demanded. "Why did Rossington choose you to send to me? How do you know him?"

Shelby lowered her eyes and closed them, keeping them closed for a long moment before opening them again and lifting her gaze to meet his. "Christopher is my brother."

Mitch narrowed his eyes. "My investigation of Christopher Rossington and his father, Adam, the original head of the Rossington organization, was thorough. Adam Rossington had only one child."

Shelby kept her gaze on Mitch's. "Adam wanted sons, not daughters. My birth certificate lists father as unknown."

"Then what you told me about your parents dying in a car crash in France was a lie?"

Slowly, Shelby nodded.

Mitch's anger went white-hot. "Your brother? You said you've been working for him for six months. This his way of bringing you into the family business?"

Shelby's face reddened with anger of her own. "He has my daughter!"

"Yeah, I got that the first time you said it." Mitch's voice was tight. "Uncle Chris babysitting while you do this job for him?"

Shelby shivered. "He is not the doting uncle. He'd never seen Sara until the night he came to my apartment in France with two of his men and took her." Shelby stopped speaking, swallowing convulsively, then went on. "He told me of your investigation of him and what he wanted me to do. He snapped his fingers and one of the men held me while the other went into my daughter's bedroom where she was sleeping and without a word, without a glance, left with her." Shelby's breathing hitched. "I went crazy, kicking and screaming. Christopher told me if I failed him, I would never see Sara again. He's not going to wait much longer." Shelby gripped her hands so tightly, her fingers whitened. "He made sure I got that message in the alley the other night."

"Rossington ordered that attack on you?"

"Yes."

Mitch had no doubt that Rossington was capable of turning on his family. But was her claim that her brother was behind the attack the truth, or another lie to make herself out the innocent victim?

"I'm terrified that Christopher will take out his anger with me on Sara," Shelby said.

She looked close to falling apart and seeing her so beaten down hit him. He had to fight the urge to take her in his arms and reminded himself that she had carried out an elaborate scheme for a vicious criminal.

She inhaled several breaths as if to steady herself and to keep from losing it completely. "Mitch, if Christopher knows you're onto him, he'll only get more closed up. He's confident now, thinking he has an edge you don't know about. Why blow that? Whatever you think of me, there's a child's life at stake here."

The pain and fear in her eyes now made Mitch feel he'd wronged her somehow. As if he could. She was Rossington's mole.

Mitch took out the untraceable phone he used for his communication with Harwick. He didn't expect Harwick to pick up and left no voicemail. Harwick would see the missed call and know to dial Mitch back when it was safe to do so.

Shelby lurched toward him. "What are you going to do?" When he didn't respond, she said, "Mitch?" Her voice was shrill.

He gave her a level look. "You don't really expect me to lay my plans out for you? After what I just found out about your relationship with Rossington?"

"That's my child."

"If there is a child."

She sucked in her breath. "If ... you think I

made Sara up?"

Mitch's voice went dangerously soft. "You've lied to me from the beginning. Why would I not think you're making this up now that your back is to the wall? I can't take anything you tell me at face value anymore."

"I'm telling you the truth."

Mitch could hear her desperation in her voice and worked to harden himself against it. Whether she was desperate because she was cornered or because she really was telling the truth about her child, he couldn't say. "You haven't told the truth since I've known you. I'd be a fool to believe anything you tell me without checking it out."

He didn't think Shelby could get any paler, but her face went a shade whiter. He gritted his teeth against going to her. He had every right to his doubt and anger.

"If you start digging around to check this out, Christopher will know. You said you did the background. Then you know Christopher is as much of a monster as our father was. Sara means nothing to him. He won't care if he hurts her. He'd do so with relish to prove his point to me." Shelby blurted that out, each word tripping over the last in her haste to get them said.

Calling himself a fool for giving her distress any consideration, Mitch said, "Rossington won't know anything. I'll be discreet."

Shelby clutched his forearm, nails digging in. "He has eyes and ears everywhere. He'll find out. Please Mitch. Please we have to do as he says."

"Rossington is no longer calling the shots here. I am. If you really do have a child and if she really is in danger, then you'll want me to confirm her existence as soon as possible. I'm your one chance at getting her back alive."

Shelby wrapped an arm tight around her middle.

"How do you and Rossington contact each other?" Mitch asked.

She hesitated, then must have thought there was no point to withholding that information. "Text messages. One asterisk. Our meeting times are during the day at the Blake Park during business hours. Not that we've met often."

Mitch held out his hand. "Your cell phone."

"I can't give you that. What if he tries to reach me? If I don't respond, he'll know something is wrong. He'll kill Sara."

"I'll let you know if he contacts you. I need to make sure you don't contact him."

Shelby shook her head slowly. "I already told you, I need to make sure he doesn't find out that you know anything about my involvement with him. We're on the same page in this."

"Until I've confirmed your story, I'll have your phone. Either that, or we drive to the station and I blow the lid on this now. First you talk to me, then the DA and after I'd bet the Feds would want to have a word with you about Rossington."

A single tear slid down Shelby's cheek. She went to her purse where she'd left it on the coffee table and returned with her cell phone. She placed it in Mitch's outstretched hand.

Fool that he was when it came to her, he watched that tear trickle unchecked down her face and felt pain he had no business feeling, given what he'd learned about her.

After Shelby handed him her phone, she retreated to one corner of the room and sank into an armchair. Drawing her legs to her chest, she wrapped her arms around them and pressed her forehead to her knees. Her fear and despair hit him as if it were his own.

Mitch's cell phone vibrated. Harwick. Mitch took the call. "I need you to check something."

"Go ahead."

Harwick's voice was loud. In the background, Mitch heard raucous laughter and Latin music blaring. "I need to know if our friend has a child stashed somewhere. A girl. She's three. Name is Sara. I need this information yesterday."

"Got it. I'll see what I can find out."

Harwick ended the call. Mitch looked back to Shelby. Her eyes were red-rimmed. She looked about to say something but her mouth opened and closed as if speech were beyond her at that moment. If she were lying about Sara, her performance was award-worthy.

"Where is Sara's father?" Mitch asked. "Do you have a husband I also don't know about?" Mitch felt jealousy at the thought of Shelby with another man. She'd had a child with another man. A life with another man.

Shelby's voice was thick with unshed tears. "He's a psychologist I met at a conference. We were never married. We haven't been together since before Sara was born. He never sees her. Fatherhood wasn't for him."

Mitch snorted. "A real prince."

Shelby didn't respond to that.

"So much makes sense now," Mitch went on. "Why you didn't give up your lease on the house. Why you wouldn't set a wedding date. What did you tell Keith about why you didn't want to accept the partnership offer?"

Her voice was low, monotone as she said, "I didn't tell him anything. He thinks I'm considering it."

Mitch's mouth firmed. "You've got this down, Shelby. Got your pretty ass covered. If I hadn't overheard you with Rossington, I never would have believed it. If anyone had come to me accusing you—anyone—I would have taken him apart and damn the consequences." The truth of that gutted him.

Shelby's lips trembled. "If there had been another way to get Sara back ..."

"If there is a Sara," he bit out. "I don't blame you for doing whatever you had to do to get your child back, but we've been together for six months. You know me. You should have told me. You should have trusted me. You didn't. You never have and that I do blame you for. You should have come to me with the truth."

Shelby's eyes blazed with anger now. "And what would you have done, Mitch? Dropped the investigation? Given me the information I needed to take back to Christopher? Of course you wouldn't have."

Mitch's jaw tightened. "If what you're saying is true, you did everything Rossington wanted of you, did that get your daughter back?" She winced and clutched her stomach as if he'd kicked her, but damn it, he was right. "Rossington will continue to use your child as a hostage to your compliance until he wrings you dry and then he'll either kill the girl or sell her. Do you know that among his many crimes, Rossington also trafficks children?"

Shelby sucked in a trembling breath.

Mitch eyed her. "You should have come to me. I would have helped you. I would have returned your child to you. Kept her safe. Kept you safe. I protect what's mine."

Her voice barely audible, she said, "I was never yours."

CHAPTER SEVEN

No, she wasn't his. She never had been and that truth cut like a knife. Mitch remembered meeting her for the first time—seeing her for the first time across the crowded room at the Blake County Hotel at the annual charity event to raise funds for the local hospital. Unbidden the memory took hold. Unwanted. He could see again her soft brown hair shimmering in the light from a chandelier above her and that instant when she must have felt his gaze and turned to face him and their eyes met. A Hollywood moment. He would have scoffed at the cliché of that but he'd felt a pull to her that he'd never felt with another woman.

He ran a hand back through his hair then stomped on the memory. Not real. None of it had been real for her. She'd been playing a role and he'd been nothing more to her than a means to an end.

If she were to be believed, that means was

getting her child back from Rossington. The jury was still out on that.

She was Rossington's *sister.* When Mitch thought of her relationship with Rossington, rage filled him. And not just for himself and how she'd duped him, but for the good men and women risking their lives to bring Rossington down. For all the people who suffered because Rossington remained free to terrorize them.

If Rossington had blackmailed her, then damn it all, she and Mitch had been together for months. He loved her. More than breath. Had made no secret of that. He would have moved heaven and earth to help her. But she hadn't come to him. Would not have come to him. If he hadn't found out himself, he'd still be in the dark. Reconciling himself to that truth left him bleeding. Anger was better than pain. He focused on that.

* * *

Shelby turned away from the condemnation in Mitch's eyes. It hurt to see that. A shield had come down closing him off to her as surely as if he'd erected a wall between them. She couldn't say she hadn't expected that, but it still hurt so much.

The rest of the day passed in what felt like slow motion. Shelby couldn't think of anything but Mitch receiving his answer about Sara. And what would happen once he did.

She tried to come up with a plan to save the situation, but her mind was paralyzed by fear and there was nothing she could think to do that would sway Mitch from his course.

By the time the call Mitch was waiting for arrived, another day had dawned and Shelby's nerves were vibrating like tuning forks. Her ears perked up as she overheard his side of the conversation.

"... so she is real," Mitch said. A pause. "Where?" He listened for some time. His expression was grim then turned angry. "This is going to happen as soon as I can pull it together. Stay close. I'll give you a warning when this is going down. Keep your head down."

Shelby had been moving closer to Mitch during his conversation and was now in front of him when he ended the call. He had his confirmation. Did that bode well or ill for the situation? And what did he mean about something "going down."

She stared up at him. "Mitch, what's happening? What do you know about Sara?"

He looked at her, his eyes flat. "That you were telling the truth about her existence."

"What are you going to do?"

With a little grunt, he turned away from her.

"Mitch, please!"

He turned back to face her. "Nothing yet. I need to make sure this isn't another set up, courtesy of you and your brother."

Shelby tasted bile at the thought. Though she acknowledged that Mitch had no reason to believe her—to trust her—she felt a flush of anger at his words. She had not wanted this. She had not wanted to do Christopher's bidding. "I've been used just as surely as you've been."

Mitch's face tensed. "Your part as a victim still remains to be seen."

* * *

Mitch pulled his cell phone from his pocket and spent the rest of the day engaged in a series of phone calls, the first of which was to Zach with a request for him to come to the house when night descended.

By the time Zach arrived, Mitch's plans were in place. Zach gave Shelby his usual warm greeting then Mitch led his friend into the kitchen.

"What's up?" Zach asked.

"I need you to stay with Shelby tonight."

Zach nodded. "No problem. You got something going down?"

Since Zach would be putting his ass on the line for him and Shelby, Mitch owed Zach the truth. He tamped down on the feeling that he was betraying Shelby and gave Zach the details on Shelby's involvement with Rossington.

Zach reared back. "What? You expect me to believe that about Shelby?"

Mitch's mouth tightened. "Believe it."

Zach ran a hand back through his hair and released a huff of breath. "Shit, man. I'm sorry."

Mitch acknowledged his friend's compassion with a quick nod.

"This has to have messed you up," Zach said gently.

Mitch didn't say anything for a moment as he beat back emotions he didn't want to deal with just now. Couldn't deal with just now. He had the information he needed. His men were ready and waiting for him. What he had going down tonight required his full concentration. He needed to keep his head in the game. But that was not the only reason he forced back what he was feeling. He looked into the living room at Shelby who stood huddled against one wall. She appeared so afraid, so vulnerable. No, not the only reason at all he forced back his feelings.

Mitch took his gaze from Shelby and back to Zach. "Rossington doesn't know that we're onto his connection with Shelby yet. Other than us, she's the only one who could alert him and I've made sure she hasn't been in contact with anyone since I confronted her."

Zach's eyes fixed on Mitch. "You think she might get in touch with him?"

The need to defend Shelby came fast and strong but he forced it down. He could not defend her. "I can't discount that possibility." Mitch's mouth soured with the vile taste of the words. "I won't risk my men walking into an ambush."

"Shelby." Zach shook his head slowly. "This is fucked up." He blew out a breath. "I'll make sure she stays put and off the phone."

With all that needed to be said, said, Mitch left the kitchen. It was time he got this night underway.

* * *

Hours earlier, Mitch had turned away from her, effectively dismissing her. He'd spent the day on the phone, making one call after another, none of which gave Shelby any information about what he was going to do, now that he knew about her and Christopher and now that he knew about Sara. Then when Zach arrived, the pair had gone off outside her hearing to speak. Whatever he'd been planning all day was happening now or soon, she could sense it.

Mitch and Zach returned to the living room. When Mitch continued to the door, Shelby knew she was right. He hadn't let her in on his plans. She knew that was deliberate on his part. He'd made it clear that he didn't trust her. She didn't blame him. He had a right to hate her. She closed her eyes riding out the pain of that, but she hoped she could still find some compassion in him. She had to know about Sara.

"What are you going to do?" Shelby's heart was beating so fast she felt her chest would burst.

Mitch turned to her. He looked at her, his blue eyes unblinking. "I'm going to bring your daughter back to you."

* * *

Mitch had gone over the information assembled on Sara's location so many times, he knew the layout of the place as intimately as if it were the body of a lover. Rossington had chosen the place well. A one-story farmhouse on the outskirts of Blake County, surrounded by open land. There was no way to mount a stealth attack. Whoever was in that farmhouse would see Mitch and his people coming as soon as they set foot on the ground.

His best chance was to go in at night when the darkness would give them some cover.

Shelby claimed that Sara was in danger. Was she? Mitch didn't know, just as he didn't know if he was leading his men into a trap.

The things he did know had him reeling. Shelby was Rossington's sister. She was working for her brother. Mitch's mouth tightened. Rossington had cost him everything. Mitch hoped with a fervor that made his mouth water that when he went through the doors of the farmhouse, the one he'd come face to face with was Rossington himself.

"All set," Mitch said quietly to the other men with him.

"Good to go," Casey Sloane responded.

Along with Sloane, Detectives Cox, Hadley, Wheeler and Fine were with Mitch for this takedown on the farmhouse. He'd kept the team deliberately small to minimize the risk of detection from the occupants of the farmhouse.

Mitch assigned Cox and Hadley to positions outside in case someone from the farmhouse made a break for it. Sloane, Wheeler and Fine would go into the farmhouse with him. Weapon drawn, Mitch broke into a sprint, leading the others across the yard.

Moonlight cast everything in silver and though the moon was a mere quarter full, the glow still felt like being under a spotlight. Somewhere in the distance an owl hooted. What sounded like all the crickets in the county were chirping.

At the farmhouse, Mitch and Sloane took the front. Fine and Wheeler made their way around back. The farmhouse was in need of a coat of paint. There'd been a storm a week ago with wind and rain and a handful of shingles littered the ground. Mitch stepped over one on his way to the front door.

His last surveillance had reported three men at the farm. There wasn't a guard posted out front now. Either Rossington didn't think there was a need for one, or whoever had been here had spotted Mitch and his team and had alerted the others. Mitch turned his face to the mic on his shoulder and whispered, "Clear" for the benefit of Fine and Wheeler. When he got the same response in return, he gave the signal to move in.

Music at low volume came from the house. A man and a woman Mitch didn't recognize sang in duet. He held up his fingers, counting to three, then kicked the weak door. The frame splintered and the door sprang open. A similar sound of wood splitting came from the back of the house. Fine and Wheeler were in as well.

As far as security went, this place was for shit, making Mitch think again that Rossington had not been concerned that anyone would come calling. Since Rossington was not a fool, he must have been very sure of Shelby, not to feel a need to secure this place like a fortress. Again the thought crossed Mitch's mind that he could be leading his men into a trap.

"Police!" Mitch yelled as he and Sloane charged inside.

The hall was long and unoccupied. A narrow

length of stained carpeting lay over an equally dirty tile floor. Pale pink flecks of paint from where the color had chipped from the walls were among the dirt.

Wheeler and Fine appeared at the end of the hall. Wheeler nodded to let Mitch and Sloane know they'd cleared the back of the house.

With Sloane going low, and Mitch high, they peered into the open living room and dining room combination and then a kitchen. A bulb above the stove gave off a faint glow. As Mitch and Sloane cleared the threshold, a mouse scurried across the counter. The kitchen was as filthy as the rest of the place and Mitch felt a tug in his heart and a wave of anger thinking of Shelby's daughter being housed here. He was more than ready for this to be done and for these assholes to be in custody.

Mitch came to a closed door. The music was coming from this room. He flattened himself against the wall and then reached over and flung the door open. It bounced off the opposite wall. He went into a crouch and surveyed the room.

The smell of sex hung in the air. A naked woman knelt in the center of a double bed. She started shrieking as soon as Mitch appeared in the doorway. Even from across the room, he could see her pupils were dilated to a point that the irises were barely visible. Clearly the woman was on something.

Ignoring her for the moment, Mitch checked under the bed and inside the closet. Whoever had been having sex with the woman wasn't in this room now.

In the time it took for Mitch and Sloane to clear the room, she hadn't blinked nor had she stopped screaming. Mitch returned to the hall.

He and Sloane passed a bathroom, the door open, and determined that no one was inside, then came to the last room.

The door was closed. No one had gotten past him or his men. If someone else was in the farmhouse, Mitch could only figure the guy was in this room and knowing he was cornered, may be planning some kind of showdown.

Fine and Wheeler joined Mitch and Sloane. Mitch kicked in the door and led the four of them into the room. A naked man, clutching a small child, was climbing out the window. Mitch wouldn't chance firing a shot with the little girl in range and pointed his gun to the ceiling. The man glanced over his shoulder, made brief eye contact with Mitch, then dropped down to the ground, disappearing from view.

Mitch spoke into his mic. "Cox. Hadley. One male on the grounds now. South side. He has the child. Hold your fire!"

Mitch ran across the room and vaulted through the window, giving chase. The same darkness that had cloaked him and his men earlier now offered the same to the man fleeing with Shelby's daughter and Mitch cursed as the man blended in with his surroundings.

The little girl wasn't crying despite the mad dash through the window and now across the farmland. No sound that would help them track the bastard who held her. But beyond Mitch's desire to get a bead on the man, he had to wonder why the child remained silent. He knew a little about kids from two nephews and could attest that when their world was disturbed the boys made sure everyone in their vicinity knew about it. Mitch's gut clenched. Why hadn't Sara let out a wail to rival the woman they'd found in the bedroom?

"Anything?" Mitch said into the mic.

"Negative," came Cox's reply that was then echoed by Hadley.

Mitch saw movement. Something separated itself from the blackness around him. He pulled his flashlight from his belt and took off in that direction.

He ate up the distance between him and the figure racing across the yard. He got close enough to tackle the other man, but again held back because of the child. He waited until the man was an arm's length away, then dropped his flashlight to the ground and grabbed him by the back of the neck with one hand and the little girl with the other.

The man released the child to confront Mitch. Mitch held her against him and jumped back to avoid a powerful right cross to his jaw. The wide beam from Mitch's flashlight provided ample light for him to get a look at his combatant. The guy looked like he lived in a gym. His head was clean shaven and the size of a melon. While Mitch would have liked to pound this guy, his first concern was the child.

He trained his weapon on the son of a bitch in front of him and said in a lethal whisper, "Freeze or I'll drop you where you stand."

Melon Head sneered. "You're going to regret this, cop. This ain't over."

Mitch bared his teeth in a chilling smile. "I'm counting on that."

Mitch gave his location to Cox and Hadley and when they arrived, he left Melon Head to them. He retrieved his flashlight and started back to the farmhouse. The little girl was dressed in only a diaper and the night air was chill. Dressed in protective gear, Mitch had no jacket to cover her with and walked briskly, keeping her tucked against his chest and encircled by his arms to ward off the cold. Shelby had said the child was three years old. She was woefully light in his arms.

Inside the farmhouse, he got his first good look at the little girl. She was too pale and too thin. An unpleasant smell rose from her small unwashed body and from a diaper that looked like it hadn't been changed in far too long. He felt anger and sadness at her condition. *Sara.* The little girl's name was Sara. He had no doubt it was Shelby's daughter he held. The shape of her face. The same shade of soft brown hair. Sara's eyes were closed but if she opened them, Mitch expected to see they were exactly a milk chocolate brown like Shelby's.

But the child's eyes remained closed. He knew she was alive because he could feel her little chest rising and falling with each breath but his heart raced with the worry of why Sara remained quiet and ... still.

Back in the small room that Sara had been held in, Mitch got his answer. An uncapped needle in a syringe lay on a nightstand beside a vial containing a sedative. Sara's little torso and arms bore too many needle marks to count. The little girl had been kept sedated. Mitch felt a flash of fury that had him wanting to level this place and the man who'd pumped the child full of the drug.

"Mitch?"

Mitch turned at the sound of Sloane's voice.

"Got a team coming in to swab this place," Sloane said.

Mitch nodded. There'd been no sign of the other two men his surveillance had spotted earlier. He didn't like that the men were unaccounted for. "Where's the woman?"

"Wheeler is with her right where we found her. Want to ask you if you want us to sit on her and the son of a bitch with her here for a while?"

"No. Have Cox and Hadley transport them both to the station. I'll be there shortly. Depending on how much contact Rossington has with his man here, or with the other two, it may take a while for him to find out that we've been here. We don't know how much time we have. Tell Cox and Hadley to be on the alert. Once Rossington knows we have his people, he'll move fast to take them out."

Mitch glanced at Sara, nestled in the crook of his arm, and came to a decision.

CHAPTER EIGHT

Many hours had passed since Mitch left. Zach was her steadfast bodyguard or was he her jailer? Shelby suspected Mitch had told Zach what was taking place tonight and her part in it. Mitch would feel Zach had a right to know what he'd involved him in. Zach hadn't spoken of it or asked any questions. He hadn't spoken to her at all. There was a tension between them that hadn't existed before. She understood it. Mitch was Zach's friend and Zach would feel that she'd wronged Mitch. She understood it and was sorry for it.

Dawn was breaking. The sky was a pink blush now. Still no word from Mitch. Was that good or bad?

Shelby had to ask. "Did Mitch give you any idea how long he'd be?"

Zach looked at her for the first time in hours. It wasn't a friendly look. "No."

She deserved his rancor but she wouldn't be

punished like this, not when it came to Sara. "Is that true? Are you holding out on me?"

Zach shook his head and his expression tightened. "I can't believe you, of all people, would ask me that."

She felt his condemnation, but straightened her shoulders. She wouldn't be put off. "That's not an answer."

His gaze sharpened. "I gave you an answer."

Zach's cell phone chimed. He took it from his belt. Shelby's breath caught.

He spoke into the phone. "Go ahead." He paused. "Got it."

Shelby was about to ask about the call, but he didn't make her wait for it.

"That was Mitch," Zach said. "He's here."

It made sense Mitch would let Zach know it was he and not an intruder coming through the door. Mitch wouldn't want to alarm Zach unnecessarily and also, Zach kept his gun primed.

"Sara?" Her little girl's name came out hoarse. Fear had a choke hold on her.

Before Zach could reply, the door opened and Mitch walked in. Alone.

Shelby stared at him. A low keening sound came from somewhere in the distance. Dimly, she realized the sound was coming from her.

Then Mitch was beside her. He clamped his hands around her arms. He bent so that his gaze was level with hers. "She's alive. She's all right."

Shelby continued to stare at him. He nodded once slowly. A tremor went through her. Her breath came out in a rush. "Where is she?"

"A clinic run by a friend of mine and Zach's."

Shelby's voice cracked. "You said Sara was all right."

"She's been in captivity for a long time. She's malnourished. Dehydrated," Mitch said softly.

Shelby closed her eyes. *Malnourished. Dehydrated.* Each word cut. "I have to see her."

Mitch nodded. "I'll take you."

* * *

Mitch led Shelby to his vehicle. At his request, Zach followed in his truck. The drive to Sara went on and on. In the months Shelby had been in Blake, she'd never ventured this far beyond the county and she had no idea where they were or how much farther they had to go.

She turned to Mitch. "Where is this place? Why didn't you take Sara to Blake County General?"

"I didn't want to risk Sara's presence there leaking. No one but us, Brock and his wife Laurel, the doctors who run the clinic, will know that Sara is there."

Mitch pulled into the driveway of a single story house and cut the engine. "This is it."

Shelby was out the door before Mitch had finished speaking and racing up the sloped driveway that led to the house.

Sara was somewhere in that house. Shelby was humming with impatience. She reached the front door and rang the bell, willing the door to open.

Mitch and Zach joined her on the small stoop as the door swung open. The man who answered had fair hair that hadn't been trimmed in several months. Shaggy and thick it curled over his nape. He was dressed in jeans that had gone white at the seams and a shirt with the sleeves rolled above the elbows.

"Brock," Mitch said.

"Hey, Mitch, come in."

Brock stepped back from the door into a small entrance. "Zach. Been too long."

Zach extended his hand to Brock. "Good to see you."

Shelby felt as if she'd waited an eternity to be reunited with Sara. Even another moment was too long a delay. She was about to interrupt Zach and Brock's conversation when Mitch drew her forward.

"Shelby," Mitch said, "this is Brock St. John."

She dispensed with any pleasantries. "How is my daughter, Doctor? Where is she?"

Brock repeated what Mitch had said about Sara being undernourished and dehydrated. "We have her on an IV and antibiotics to fight off infection. Mitch found a vial where Sara was being held that contained a sedative. We found a number of punctures on her torso and thighs. It looks like Sara spent a good deal of her captivity sedated. She's weak and going to need some time to recover. I want to keep her here for a while."

Shelby's heart broke for what her daughter had endured. "How long?"

"At least a few days. After that we'll reassess her condition. Mitch gave me a rundown of your situation. Keeping her here for a while will also serve to keep her hidden." One corner of Brock's mouth lifted in a small, compassionate smile.

"She's down this hall."

He led the way down a narrow corridor. An addition had been built onto the back of the house that held several small rooms. Most of them were occupied and dimly lit. Shelby could hear the hums and beeps of medical equipment.

Brock turned into one room that was painted a soft yellow. Four cribs were set up but only one was occupied. The one that Sara was in.

"I'll leave you to visit," Brock said.

Shelby hadn't seen Sara since the night Christopher's man took her away. Tears filled her eyes, fell, then her eyes filled again as she made her way across the room. Her movement was jerky. Her legs wobbled like bowling pins and she was now trembling from head to toe.

Sara was asleep. She was dressed in a clean pink nightie and booties that smelled like fresh lemons. Sara herself had recently been bathed and her skin and hair smelled of baby powder and baby shampoo.

Her face was smaller than Shelby recalled. Her skin looked as pale as porcelain and just as fragile.

Shelby blinked more tears and touched her fingertip to her daughter's soft cheek. Her beautiful little girl remained asleep. Shelby wanted to hold her more than she wanted to see the next sunrise. She carefully lowered one side of the crib and placed her arms around her child.

* * *

Mitch watched Shelby from the hall. Seeing her heartbreak was almost his undoing.

Zach came up beside him.

"Any problems getting Sara out?" Zach asked.

Mitch turned away from Shelby and to Zach. "No."

"Rossington won't take this lying down."

"Yeah. I'm wondering how much time we have before he learns we breached his farmhouse and have one of his men and a woman in custody. Our surveillance told us there were three men there. We only found the one."

"The other two might have taken a night off for themselves and your surveillance missed them leaving."

"It's possible. I'm having the place watched. If they return, they'll be picked up."

Zach raised a brow. "But what you're thinking is the men did slip by the surveillance and are on their way to tell Rossington what went down."

"Yeah." Mitch glanced at his watch.

"You need to be someplace?"

"I need to talk to the two who had Shelby's daughter. I need them to name Rossington."

Zach grunted. "Rossington will kill them. Their only chance is to cut a deal with the State."

"The way they kept Sara." Mitch apprised Zach of the condition he'd found her in, then sneered. "It burns my ass these animals are going to cut a deal and we're going to end up protecting them."

"The greater good," Zach said but there was anger in his tone as well.

Mitch turned away from Zach at the approach of footsteps. Mitch had assigned Wheeler and Fine to remain at the clinic. They stopped when they reached him. He introduced them to Zach and the men shook hands. Wheeler and Fine were on their way to the kitchen for coffee and continued down the hall.

Mitch turned to Zach again. "I need you to stay with Shelby. Take her home when she's ready and wait until I get there."

"Whatever you need, you got it."

"Thanks. I'm heading over to the station. Call me when you leave here."

Zach nodded.

* * *

Mitch left Zach and made his way down the hall. Wheeler and Fine would remain at the farmhouse to protect Sara, Brock, Laurel, and their patients for as long as Sara was with them and there was a chance that her presence would bring trouble to Brock's door.

Shelby's information about Sara was true. She really did have a daughter and her daughter had been held captive by a man who worked for Rossington. It did appear that Shelby was the victim, coerced into cooperating with Rossington to save her child.

But had Rossington needed to force her to help him? He was her brother, after all.

Mitch curled his lip in a snarl. Flesh and blood and all that. Maybe the victim in this—the only victim—was Sara. Mitch would never believe that Shelby had known her daughter was being mistreated. If she'd trusted her brother with her child, then she'd made one hell of a mistake.

It could have gone down that way and

Rossington had not forced Shelby at all. Mitch's suspicions, his doubts were certainly justified. She was an accomplished liar, had lied to him convincingly for months about everything. Who she was. That she was spying for her brother. About her love for him.

There was bitterness with that thought and pain. *Fuck.* His lips thinned in an expression of self-directed anger that despite what he now knew about her, he could still feel pain over her. He needed to get his head straight. He couldn't afford to be off his game now. He had a job to do— get Rossington. That was all that mattered now.

He reached the building that housed the police station and went to the interrogation rooms. Sloane was already there. He looked wrecked after a day and the better part of a night without sleep. He'd be going off shift soon but right now, Sloane sucked back a mouthful of coffee like it was life-sustaining. While Sloane brought Mitch up to date on the status of the two people apprehended at the farm, Mitch got a cup of coffee for himself.

"Guy's name is Randall Ashling," Sloane said. "No priors. Not even a parking ticket. As to the woman, we got a sheet on her. Possession. Solicitation." Sloane stopped walking when they came to one of the doors that led to an interview room. "They're ready when you are, Mitch. Woman's in room four. Ashling's in five."

Mitch wanted to speak with the woman first. He glanced at the sheet Sloane handed him for her name. Dorothy Simms. On the street she went by the name Amber Liquid.

The woman seated on the orange plastic chair in the interview room didn't look like she'd inspire thoughts of lust. He'd had a quick glimpse of her at the farm, and now took a closer inspection. The bright fluorescents didn't do her any favors. Every one of the small marks that dotted her sallow complexion showed under the harsh lighting. The roots of her hair were an inky black, in contrast to the platinum blond dye job, and a couple of inches thick. Her collar bones protruded from her skin. The woman looked like she hadn't eaten—or eaten well—in a very long time. Food wasn't likely a priority, judging the needle track marks in her arms. She sat picking at them. She lifted her gaze to his. Mascara had smudged beneath her eyes, eyes grown dull as her high wore off, and watched him warily, like a doe caught in a rifle's cross hairs.

"I'm Chief Turner, Amber. Do you know why you're here?"

Amber didn't blink, but continued to stare at him. "Look, I already told the other cop. I wasn't doing nothing wrong. I was just on a date. Dating ain't illegal."

"Where did you hook up with Ashling?"

She shrugged. "I was in the city, ah, shopping. He looked like a nice guy. When he invited me back to his place, I went. That's it."

"He tell you what he does for a living?"

"We weren't talking." She grinned at Mitch. "Know what I mean?"

"You got anybody to verify that you met Ashling for the first time tonight?"

Amber swallowed and licked her lips, now less

sure of herself. "Don't need that."

"Yeah, you do." Mitch crossed his arms. "If I can't find someone to corroborate your claim that you met Ashling tonight, then I'm going to conclude that you knew him before tonight and that you were in on the kidnapping of the child we found at the farmhouse."

The pulse in Amber's neck began to throb visibly. "What kid! I don't know nothing about a kid. I never saw a kid. I just went there to do my job. No way I'd kidnap a kid. I would never hurt a kid. I got a kid of my own."

"So far you're not convincing me."

"Okay. Okay. Listen. I'm a working girl. I'll cop to that." She held up a hand, fingers splayed. The dark blue polish was chipped on several nails. "If I knew this guy was a kidnapper, do you think I would have gotten involved with him?"

Mitch kept his gaze on hers and repeated his earlier question. "Ashling tell you what he does for a living?"

"Nah. I figured had to be something that paid well the way he was waving around the Ben Franklins. I figured a guy with that kind of green might become a regular customer. Might have friends. Repeat business. Referrals." She shrugged. "A girl's got to look out for herself." She gnawed her bottom lip, chewing off the last of red lipstick. "I didn't know nothing about no kid. You got to believe me."

Mitch did believe her. She was a hooker Ashling had picked up for the night. She could give them nothing on Rossington.

He turned away from Amber and led Sloane to

112

the room that held Ashling. Ashling was hunched over the table in the small room, his head in his hands. His head shot up when Mitch entered and his gaze darted from Sloane to Mitch. Gone was the combative guy who'd challenged Mitch outside the farmhouse. Ashling's high had worn off and the man now looked uncertain and afraid.

"We have you for kidnapping," Mitch said, getting right to it. "The way it stands now, you'll be going away for a long time."

Ashling jutted out his trembling chin and attempted a brave stare. "I got nothing to say till my lawyer gets here. He'll get me off. I won't go to jail."

"Oh, you'll go to prison, all right. If you live long enough."

Ashling blanched and sweat popped on his brow. "Like I said, I'll wait for my lawyer." His voice was low and shook.

The man was too afraid to turn on Rossington. Mitch would give him another fear. "Okay. Then we're done here. We'll just take you to lock up to wait for your lawyer. Put him in gen pop, Sloane."

Sloane lifted a shoulder and a crease appeared between his brows. "You sure you want me to put him there, Chief?"

Before Mitch could answer, Ashling asked, "Why? What's wrong with gen pop?"

Mitch gave Ashling a steady stare. "The men in there don't like children to be abused. Most of them take it personally if someone does harm to a child."

"I didn't do nothin' to that kid."

Mitch gave Ashling a deadly look. "You kept

that little girl drugged. Barely fed. In her own filth. The men you're about to meet won't like how you treated her. Sloane, we're done here."

Sloane reached for Ashling. Ashling pulled back. "He'll kill me, man! He'll kill me!"

Mitch got into Ashling's face. "Who?"

Ashling paled then shook his head. "I can't. I can't say anything. He'll kill me. You don't know him. If I say anything, I'm as good as dead."

"If I were you, I'd worry about what's going to happen to you while you're waiting for your lawyer to get here."

Sloane reached for Ashling again. Ashling screeched and jumped back, toppling the chair and landing on the floor with it. "You can't put me in with those animals!"

Mitch gave him a feral smile. "Watch me."

Ashling blanched. Sweat dripped down his face. He held up his trembling palms to ward Sloane off. "Okay. Okay. I was keeping the kid for Rossington. I don't know what it was all about. Just that I was told to keep her."

"How long you been working for Rossington?"

"A couple years."

Mitch crossed his arms. "What do you do for him? Amber said you had a wad of cash. I'm thinking I have one of Rossington's lieutenants here."

"No. No." Ashling shook his head quickly. "It was all show for the whore. I'm no lieutenant. I just do low level stuff. Like this. I'm no heavyweight. He just needed someone to babysit the kid."

"Rossington himself gave you the order?"

When Ashling hesitated, Mitch gave in to his anger. "Take him."

"No! Please! No! It was Rossington," Ashling screamed.

Mitch could smell the foul odor of Ashling's fear sweat. He thought of how afraid little Sara must have been while under this son of a bitch's care and it was all he could do to keep the table between himself and Ashling. "Say. It."

"Okay. Okay. Mr. Rossington himself told me to watch the kid."

"How much longer you think that little girl could have lived the way you were keeping her? Did Rossington tell you to kill her?"

"Nobody said nothin' about killing a kid. I wasn't going to kill a kid." Ashling was blubbering now with tears streaming down his cheeks. "I wasn't going to kill a kid no matter if Mr. Rossington said so. You have to believe me." His eyes got so wide they looked about to pop out of his head. "I never would have killed a kid. I was just the babysitter. I was just the babysitter."

Mitch's shoulders tightened with the desire to rip Ashling's head from his shoulders. He turned away from the other man and left the room before the urge overtook him and he did just that.

Out in the hall, Sloane said, "I'll get on the warrant for Rossington."

"Let me know when it comes in." Mitch felt his features harden. This had become personal with Rossington. "I want to bring that son of a bitch in myself."

CHAPTER NINE

Mitch left the police station. The day was gray, promising rain. A cool breeze scattered petals that had fallen from flowers planted along the walkway.

It was minutes before nine a.m. He crossed the parking lot to his own vehicle. A man and woman who worked in administration hurried by him making their way to the station to start their work day. Mitch exchanged nods with them.

Zach hadn't called. Mitch took out his cell phone and called Zach.

"Where are you?" Mitch asked when Zach answered his phone. There was no sound other than Zach's voice coming through the line to give away his location.

"Still at Brock's," Zach said. "Shelby isn't going to budge from Sara's side."

"How is Sara? Any change?"

"Brock says she's stable."

The little girl was holding her own. Mitch was

profoundly glad of it.

"Where do things stand with Rossington?" Zach asked.

Mitch's grip on the phone tightened at the mention of that bastard's name. "Ashling gave him up. We're waiting for the warrant."

"Let me know when you have him."

Mitch grunted. "I'll be in touch."

Mitch ended the call. It had been over twenty-four hours since he'd slept and showered. He should be feeling the lack of sleep but he was too pumped, too wired and sleep was the last thing on his mind.

He'd based Rossington's warrant on Sara's kidnapping. Mitch had used Ashling to nail Rossington. Ashling's statement to the DA hadn't named Shelby because Ashling didn't know anything about her or about the child he was holding. So far Mitch had left Shelby out of it with the DA. That wouldn't last forever. Eventually, she'd have to tell her story and the truth of her involvement with her brother would come out.

Mitch intended to keep that from happening for as long as he could. If Harwick got them what they needed to pin Sara's confinement on Rossington, or unearthed other prosecutable evidence of that bastard's many crimes, maybe Mitch could keep Shelby out of this completely. He didn't want to explore why he should want that and cut off the thought.

He focused on another thought instead. Very soon he'd have Rossington in custody. Mitch clenched his jaw. He couldn't wait.

* * *

Four days passed and there was no sign of Rossington. The son of a bitch had gone to ground. Mitch was running on a short fuse that was getting shorter with each hour that failed to produce the man. He stared hard out his office window at the dark night. *Where the hell are you, Rossington?*

The thought gnawed at Mitch as he left his office and rode the elevator down to the building's below-ground level where the holding cells were located. Randall Ashling was being transported from the cell to a safe house. Ashling would remain in protective custody until Rossington was brought to trial and Ashling was required to give his testimony.

Ashling was in the first cell on the block. Sloane was waiting outside Ashling's cell when Mitch arrived, along with two other detectives who were going to assist with the transport. The men greeted Mitch with solemn nods.

Mitch addressed Sloane. "All set?"

Sloane and the two male detectives, Branson and Swartz, wore protective vests. Sloane handed a vest to Mitch.

"I oversaw every detail myself," Sloane said. "We're good to go."

Mitch put the vest on then inclined his head to Sloane. "Open the cell."

Mitch entered the holding cell. Beneath his own protective vest, Ashling was dressed in the stained jeans and faded T-shirt he'd had on when he'd given his statement about Rossington first to Mitch and then to the DA. A rank odor hung in the air from the clothing and from Ashling himself.

Ashling was pacing, walking from one end of the cell to the other. A sheen of sweat coated his shaved head and glistened under the harsh ceiling bulb. He came to a stop in the center of the cell and looked at Mitch. Mitch saw nerves in Ashling's eyes, nerves and fear.

Mitch eyed Ashling. "This is how we're going to do this. You're going to walk out of this cell with me. My detective is going to cuff you, then you're going to leave this building with me and the police escort I've arranged. You're going to be as docile as a lamb."

Ashling ran a shaky hand over his scalp. "You aren't gonna have trouble from me. I want nothing more than to be gone from here where Rossington can't find me."

"Then we're in agreement."

Mitch led Ashling out to the hall where Swartz handcuffed him. Mitch's detectives and Mitch himself closed ranks around Ashling so the man was shielded on all sides. Mitch took the lead, then gave the order to, "Move out."

Ashling's transport had been kept under wraps with only Mitch and the detectives assisting aware of what was going down. Even Ashling himself hadn't known he was being moved tonight until ten minutes ago.

Mitch reached the rear exit of the station and pushed the door open. It was after three in the morning. He'd chosen this time when most of

Blake County's residents were off the streets and there would be fewer distractions. The door opened to a gravel parking lot. Lamp poles provided bright light, giving him a full view of the area.

The ground was damp from an afternoon rainfall. Small puddles filled the ruts on the lot. The temperature was warmer than it had been in several days and the crickets and cicadas that had gone quiet due to the cold now made themselves heard.

The unmarked sedan Sloane would be driving, with Mitch riding shotgun, was parked near the door as Mitch had ordered. Mitch had also ordered that the vehicle be delivered at this time and not before, rather than be left to sit unclaimed to draw attention and speculation.

Sloane placed one hand on his weapon, holstered at his shoulder, and the other on Ashling's forearm. He unlocked the car door and placed Ashling in the back then went around the vehicle to the driver's side.

Swartz and Branson joined Ashling in the car, one detective on either side of him. As Mitch was about to get into the sedan, he saw movement. It was Britton, one of the attendants who signed out vehicles for police use, and who had signed out this one to Sloane. Britton was striding quickly off the lot. Where the hell was the man going? He'd been to the station enough times to know there was nothing but open field where he was headed.

Sloane got behind the wheel and slammed the car door. Britton stumbled on the gravel and went down on one knee. He glanced back over his shoulder. Mitch saw the man's face in the light from the lamps. Britton looked terrified.

Britton's gaze shot to the sedan. He must have felt Mitch's stare because an instant later he looked to Mitch. Their gazes held then Britton's eyes darted back to the vehicle. He sprang to his feet and ran.

Mitch narrowed his eyes at the fleeing Britton then looked to the car as Britton had. Mitch's heart began beating double time. "Sloane!" Mitch shouted. "No!"

Sloane turned the key in the ignition. The sedan exploded.

* * *

It was after three a.m. Shelby stood at Sara's crib, her arms across the raised sides, looking down at her sleeping daughter. The ceiling light was dimmed but still bright enough that Shelby could see the orange, purple and lemon yellow animal characters on the comforter that covered Sara, and see Sara herself.

They'd been at Brock's for four days. In that little time, Sara's skin was regaining its healthy pink color. She was gaining weight. Her cheeks were no longer hollowed-out but were plumping. Her little girl was recovering and back with her. Shelby felt a surge of emotion. Her daughter really was here.

Sara may not have survived much longer. Shelby shuddered thinking how close it had been. But she hadn't lost Sara. Shelby brought herself back from that dark place. She hadn't lost her daughter.

Because of Mitch.

You should have come to me. I would have returned your child to you. Shelby hadn't been able to get what he'd said out of her mind. Was he right in telling her that? Should she have gone to him about Christopher long before she was found out? Would Sara have been saved that much earlier? Tears burned Shelby's throat thinking Sara could have been spared so much if she'd told Mitch the truth. She bowed her head, squeezed her eyes shut, riding out that pain. Mitch told her she should have trusted him. After her encounter with Christopher's messenger, in Mitch's bed, in his arms, she'd almost told him, but at the last pulled back. He blamed her for her lack of trust. He had no way of knowing she'd learned very early in life not to trust anyone.

Thinking of Mitch brought a new wave of pain. He'd never been hers. She'd told herself that over and over but in some small corner of her mind she'd hoped that someday, someway, he could be. She exhaled, her breath shaky. She no longer harbored that hope. Mitch would never love her again.

Shelby heard footsteps behind her. Brock entered the room.

"Hey," Brock said in a near whisper.

Shelby took a moment to regain her shaky composure then faced Brock. She wasn't surprised to see him awake at this hour. A new patient, a small boy suffering from severe burns, had come in yesterday morning. Shelby didn't know all the particulars, but both Brock and Laurel had looked grim. Given what Shelby had observed of the doctors and had experienced with their care of Sara, she knew they would be closely monitoring the new arrival and forgoing their own rest.

"How's the little boy?" Shelby asked. She didn't think she needed to clarify which patient she spoke of.

His mouth turned down at the corners. "Alive."

"If any two people can make sure he stays that way, it's you and Laurel," Shelby said.

Brock rubbed a hand over his face. He widened his eyes owl-like, fighting sleep. His mouth formed a thin line. "I'm not going to give that boy up without one hell of a fight."

"He's lucky to have you. As is Sara. I haven't thanked you and Laurel for all you've done for my daughter."

Brock's gaze lowered to Sara. He smiled gently. "She's going to be just fine." He returned his focus to Shelby. "I didn't stop by to talk about Sara. I'm here about you."

Shelby raised her eyebrows. "Oh?"

"I'm worried about you."

"I appreciate your concern, Brock, but I'm fine. Now that I have Sara back and she's going to be all right, I'm more than fine."

"Mitch didn't give me the details on your situation but I think it's safe to say you have a lot on your mind." Brock reached into the breast pocket of the shirt he wore and took out a small plastic pill container. He held it up between his thumb and forefinger. "To help you turn off. I just gave you a few to catch you up on your rest and to help activate your natural sleep patterns so you won't need any more of these. I've noticed you aren't sleeping much."

Shelby took the bottle. A handful of pills showed through the clear plastic.

"I'll leave you to get some rest," Brock said and left the room.

Brock was right, she hadn't been sleeping much or deeply, but had been sustaining on snatches of sleep. All she could allow herself. He'd been kind to bring her the pills. She didn't want to disparage his kindness and throw them out, but neither would she take any of them and be left senseless. Once Christopher found out that she'd betrayed him to Mitch, he'd come after her. She needed to be ready to move. She tossed the bottle in her purse.

* * *

When Sloane's hand moved to the sedan's ignition, Mitch knew he'd shouted the warning too late and dove back into the building through the still-open door. As the door closed behind him, he flattened himself on the floor. The blast shook the building. Sheetrock, ceiling tiles and fluorescent tubing fell on him. Mitch raised his hands to cover his head then belly crawled across the floor, now covered by debris.

At the door, he vaulted to his feet and ran back outside. A ball of flame burned where the sedan had been. Chunks of metal and bits of car parts littered the parking lot. The roar of the flames rose above all other sound.

He raised a hand to his eyes to shield them from the bright light of the flames and started toward the fire. The heat hit him like a living thing, pushing him back. He moved forward again only to be driven back once more. Twice more, he tried. Twice more he was forced to retreat.

Shouts came from behind him. Sirens wailed. Mitch took a sharp breath and bent over, bracing his hands on his thighs. He closed his eyes. Sloane, Swartz, Branson and Ashling were gone.

CHAPTER TEN

Mitch had been over it a thousand times in his head but no matter how many times he went through it, he didn't like it any better. In fact, if possible, he hated it more. But it all came down to one thing. He was fresh out of options.

He slammed the door to his SUV and crossed the driveway to Brock's clinic. A half-moon lit his path as he made his way to Brock's front door. He'd waited for nightfall to come to see Shelby, hoping another alternative would present itself. Nothing had. So here he was. At a quarter of midnight.

Brock answered Mitch's knock.

"Hey, Mitch."

Brock ran a hand back through his mussed hair. His eyes looked heavy, either Mitch had awakened him or Brock hadn't slept in some time. "Sorry for the hour, Brock. I need to talk with Shelby."

Brock stepped back from the door. "Sure.

Come in. We put a cot for her in Sara's room. I imagine she's in there. You remember the way?"

"Yeah, thanks."

Mitch made his way down the hall. Wheeler was seated outside Sara's room, eyes down as he read a newspaper.

"Evening, Chief." Wheeler set the paper on the floor by the chair leg and an empty coffee mug.

"Everything been good here?" Mitch asked.

"Quiet as a church during penance."

Mitch nodded then entered the room that housed Sara. The little girl was asleep on her stomach. One tiny hand curled into a fist. Her small back rose and fell slowly with each inhalation and exhalation. Night and day to how he'd found her. He bit down hard on his back teeth to quell a sudden rush of anger. He was going to make sure Rossington ended his days in a cage.

Shelby was awake, laying on a cot beside Sara's crib. She was facing her daughter and hadn't yet noticed Mitch. She looked fresh from a bath. Her cheeks were flushed. Her soft brown hair had a tendency to curl when left to dry and now formed soft spirals that fell to her shoulders. Seeing her like this made him want to lay her back on that cot and show her just how beautiful she was like he'd done so many times.

His lower body tightened, becoming painful with the desire to act on what he'd been thinking. He stomped on the thought. She wasn't his. All the times he'd done just that, made love to her until they were both sated and neither of them had the strength to move, had never been real for her. Each kiss she'd deepened, each caress she'd returned had all been an act. That truth sliced him open.

Forcing his thoughts back to the reason he was here, he addressed Shelby. "We need to talk."

She turned to face him then sucked in a breath and rose off the cot. She reached out to him as if she were going to touch him, but stopped herself, curled her fingers, and let her hand fall away. "Your head? Are you all right?"

Something had fallen on him following the car bomb and struck his brow, tearing the skin almost to the bone. He had a Frankenstein look going on from all the stitches. "I'm fine. Let's talk in the hall."

Mitch stepped back for her to walk ahead of him. Shelby took her robe off the end of the cot and swung it on as she crossed the room.

In the hall, she turned to him. "What's happened?"

Though Mitch would brief Wheeler and Fine, he wanted to speak with Shelby now without an audience and turned to Wheeler. "Would you give us a minute?"

Wheeler got to his feet and hoisted the mug. "No problem." He smiled. "I could use more coffee."

After Wheeler left Mitch said, "We had one of the men who was keeping Sara in custody. I told you that."

"Yes."

"This asshole, Ashling, named Rossington as the one he was holding Sara for and we went ahead and issued an arrest warrant. We haven't been able to enforce it. Rossington has gone under. We can't find him but he made his presence known yesterday. We were transporting Ashling to a secure location. He and three of my detectives were blown up in a car bomb."

Shelby's hand went to her mouth. "Oh, God."

Mitch said nothing, feeling the loss of his men.

Shelby squeezed her eyes shut only to open them an instant later. "You said 'we'. You were there, as well?"

"Yeah. I hadn't gotten into the car yet."

"Mitch."

Shelby spoke his name through lips that now trembled. She pressed the back of her hand against them as if to still them, but her hand was also trembling. Was this the first time she'd seen up close what her brother was capable of? If so, let her here all of it.

"I hadn't gotten into the car yet," Mitch repeated, "but Sloane had."

Shelby knew Sloane from work events and had accompanied Mitch to the recent Christening of Sloane's third son. That's why he'd mentioned Sloane and not Swartz and Branson. He wanted her to feel what had happened. She hadn't put that bomb in the car but part of him blamed her just the same. Her lies had set this chain of events in motion.

"I'm so sorry about Sloane and the other officers," she said softly.

The flush in her cheeks drained leaving her a pasty white and she released a breath that shook as badly as the rest of her. He'd wanted her to feel that bombing, but now that she was, he felt like the world's biggest bastard.

This wasn't what he came here for. His anger was simmering just below the surface and he had to cool that burn and do what he needed to do.

Mitch went on. "The guy who planted the car bomb was killed in a hit and run within minutes of the bomb going off. Rossington cleaned house." While Mitch wouldn't mourn for Britton, Britton would have provided the link to Rossington that Mitch needed. "Without Ashling's testimony, we have nothing." Yeah, he'd been over it a thousand times, but still had trouble getting the words out. Hated like hell what he was about to say. "I need you to come back with me, Shelby. Testify against him." After seeing the way Sara had been treated, Mitch knew Rossington had no regard for family and had to consider that he might come after Shelby. Mitch had hoped to leave her out of it and use Ashling to get Rossington. With Ashling dead, that was no longer an option.

A light dimmed in her eyes. "Yes, of course you'd want that." She cupped her hands around her elbows, drawing herself in tight. "I can't do that."

"Can't or won't?" The words came out sharp. So much for cooling his anger.

Anger flared in her eyes now. "Can't. I have to get out of here. I have to take Sara and get far away from Christopher."

"Is that the real reason or is it that you won't testify against your brother?" Mitch made no effort to keep his suspicion out of his voice.

She lifted her chin. "My brother is a monster.

He is no less of one to his family. Christopher is the last person on this earth I would protect. As much as I want to see him pay for everything he's done, I can't be the one to bring that about. If it were just me ..." She shook her head. "But it isn't. I have Sara. I have to protect Sara."

Mitch stared hard at her. "If that's the truth then you'll want to make sure Rossington isn't ever able to get to her."

Sadness filled Shelby's eyes. "It doesn't matter what I tell you, you're not going to believe me. I can't debate this with you. If Christopher hasn't found out yet that I'm the one who betrayed him to you, then he soon will and when he does, he'll come after me. If he finds me, he'll find Sara. We have to disappear. I know you're the chief of police, but Mitch, let me make Sara safe."

Was she missing something that was right in front of her or just grasping at anything to sway him? "If he thinks you betrayed him and are now cooperating with me, he'll expect you're going to testify against him."

Shelby closed her eyes briefly then opened them to show a bleakness that hadn't been there an instant earlier. "It's done then. You never intended for me to have a choice."

She looked defeated and it struck him to his core. He wanted to tell her that nothing had been done. That the only one who knew of her association with Rossington, other than him, was Zach. That he hadn't told the DA one word about her. He wanted to tell her if he had another way to nail her brother to the wall, he'd take it.

But he couldn't say any of that. He didn't

know if her brother was a threat to her. Would Rossington believe she'd betrayed him deliberately and not because she'd been found out? Would the how of it make a difference to that son of a bitch? Mitch didn't know, but if there was even a chance that Rossington would come after her, Mitch would do everything in his power to make sure he could never hurt Shelby. Over his dead body would Rossington hurt Shelby. She wanted to go off on her own, but Mitch would not leave her unprotected and at that bastard's mercy.

"I can't let you go," he said simply.

Shelby's eyes grew wide and pleading. "I know I wronged you and you have no reason to do anything for me but you have to let me leave with Sara. Please, Mitch. Please!"

Her pleading was almost his undoing. He leaned in close to her, closer than he'd been to her since he'd discovered her with Rossington, and willed her to see the truth in his eyes. "This isn't about us. Let's be clear about that. What went down with us has nothing to do with why I told you, you can't leave. If you're telling me the truth, then you know exactly what your brother is capable of. You can't keep Sara safe from him. You can't keep yourself safe." Mitch's voice hardened. "I can and I will."

* * *

Shelby stared into Mitch's eyes, then lowered her gaze and wrapped her arms around herself. She'd changed Sara's last name so it was different from hers. With Sara's father out of her life, that had been the easiest thing she'd done. Next, she arranged for her daughter to board at pre-schools. No one who knew her ever heard her speak of a child or saw her with one. There'd been long periods of time when she didn't dare go to her daughter and the separation had left her feeling empty. But keeping Sara a secret from Christopher was worth any cost and her actions kept her child hidden from him for the first thirty months of her life.

It hadn't been easy trying to keep ahead of her brother. Christopher pursued her relentlessly. He enjoyed playing cat to her mouse. Each time she moved and settled in a new place, believed she was out from under his thumb, he'd appear. Not at first, not right away. He kept her on edge, never knowing when he would show up. But he always did. And when he did, he'd leave no doubt that her freedom from him was an illusion.

She didn't know where she'd tripped up, six months ago. How he'd found out about Sara. All she knew was that he had and her worst nightmare had been realized. If she thought she could take Sara now and disappear, go where Christopher wouldn't ever find them, she had only to recall that horrific night when he came to her apartment in France and took her child. Mitch was right. She could no longer keep Sara safe from Christopher on her own.

If her brother didn't already know she'd betrayed him to Mitch, he soon would. He wouldn't permit a threat to him to continue to exist. No matter how far or how fast she ran now, he would find her. He would never stop pursuing her. And when he found her, she had no doubt he'd make her wish for death long before he killed her. What would he do to Sara?

"Shelby?"

Mitch's voice startled her from her thoughts. The hair on the back of her neck had risen and her mouth had gone dry as dust with fear. Mitch must have noticed a change in her. He reached out and gripped her chin, lifting it so she would look him in the eye. He held her in place so she could look no where else but at him.

A line on his forehead deepened and his gaze went laser sharp. "What are you thinking? What's made you look like you just saw the devil?"

That was a fitting description of her brother. She shuddered.

"Shelby. Talk to me."

She inhaled several deep breaths in an effort to control her emotions. "I know you can protect Sara. I know I can trust you to keep her safe."

Mitch nodded slowly, never taking his eyes from hers. "Not just Sara. I'll protect you too."

Yes, he'd make sure his witness remained safe to testify. It shouldn't hurt that she meant no more to him than that, but it did. "I'll talk to the DA. How do we do this?"

"I'll set up a meeting for tonight."

She nodded and he left her to make the necessary arrangements. She changed out of her night clothes. She dressed in jeans and a loose-fitting pullover, feeling chilled despite the mild weather. She'd been dressed for some time and standing over Sara in the crib when Mitch returned to the room.

He joined her at the crib. "Ready?" He pitched his voice low.

Sara had awakened briefly then drifted off to sleep once again. Shelby leaned over the rail and kissed Sara's cheek softly then raised the rail carefully, not wanting to awaken her daughter. Sara slept on.

"I'm ready," Shelby said.

While Mitch was right that she could no longer protect Sara on her own, he'd made it clear she wasn't free to leave. He'd mentioned once charging her with obstruction. Was that charge enough for him to force her to remain? Shelby didn't know and wasn't in a position to consult a lawyer right now since she was in hiding. Yes, she and Sara needed Mitch's protection, but protecting her served him. He had nothing on Christopher without her testimony and needed her to make his case.

She had no choice but to stay. Soon she'd be telling all to the DA. Would the DA decide she'd be just as safe from Christopher in a jail cell? Sara was being well taken care of at Brock's. There was no reason Shelby had to be with her. Certainly no reason that would sway an officer of the court. By the end of this meeting, Shelby could very well find herself a guest of the state.

It was after four o'clock in the morning when Mitch turned onto the road that would take them to their meeting with Blake County District Attorney Derek Canyon. Mitch had arranged to meet at an old church back in Blake. The double church doors were unlocked, left open to the homeless and the poor. Mitch pushed open one of them and held it for Shelby to precede him inside. Two men were asleep in the pews. Neither man stirred.

The interior was dim. Candles flickered by the altar, providing the only light and casting small shadows. The scent of the wax hung in the air.

"Canyon's meeting us downstairs," Mitch said.

He led her past a door marked "Restroom" to another that took them into the church's basement. Shelby knew Derek casually through Mitch. They'd conversed and exchanged pleasantries at police and city functions that she'd attended with Mitch. This was far from the casual and social small talk they'd exchanged in the past and her stomach felt as if it were tied in knots.

In the basement, Derek was seated at a square wooden table. Of medium build and height with perpetually wind-blown hair, he was being touted as the next political hopeful. Derek stood and the men exchanged brief greetings. Shelby hung back, giving them a moment and taking one for herself. Yes, she knew Derek, but she didn't know him like this. He wasn't a friend tonight.

Derek turned to Shelby. "Hello, Shelby."

She worked to keep a tremor from her voice. "Derek."

In addition to the wooden table, there were two ladder-back chairs in the center of the room. An assortment of cardboard boxes were pushed against one wall. A furnace backed against another. Derek pulled one of the chairs away from the table for Shelby and she slowly lowered herself onto the seat.

Derek got right to the point as he resumed his own seat. "Mitch told me you have information that will enable us to prosecute Christopher Rossington."

Mitch moved to stand behind her. To someone else, it would have been perceived as a show of protection. But Mitch had brought her here. He certainly wasn't seeking to protect her from Derek.

Shelby gripped the strap of her purse. Her tone was cool despite her nerves when she said a simple, "Yes."

Derek's eyes were avid on her. It was obvious he was anxious to hear what she had to tell him. His scrutiny put her more on her guard. The knot in her stomach tightened.

"I understand that Rossington is your brother," Derek said.

Shelby nodded. The movement was slow, stiff.

"Why don't you start at the beginning when your brother first asked you to infiltrate Mitch's investigation?"

Shelby's heart picked up its pace. She told him of Christopher's visit to her in France and subsequent abduction of Sara.

"How did Rossington find out about the investigation?" Derek asked.

Shelby shook her head. "I don't know."

"He didn't mention that?"

"No."

"Did you ask him about it?"

She stared at him. "My daughter had just been taken from me. I wasn't thinking about probing

Christopher for information."

"Okay. What did you talk with him about when you met?"

Shelby rubbed her forehead with enough force to scrape away the skin. "We only met a couple of times. I had no information for him. The meetings didn't last long and always ended the same with him telling me that if I failed him, I'd never see Sara again." Even in memory, those instances with Christopher still terrified her. But Sara was safe at Brock's. Shelby took a steadying breath and repeated to herself: Sara was safe.

"Shelby, you're off our books," Derek said. "We didn't know a thing about you. The fact that we didn't would have made you very valuable to your father when he was alive and make you valuable to your brother now."

"Derek," Mitch said, his tone dangerously low.

An icy coldness seeped into her. "I was never valuable to my father or brother." The admission shamed her. Years later, and a career devoted to counseling the abused about their feelings of shame, but she'd never overcome her own.

Derek regarded her steadily. "Is this the first time you've helped your brother? Have you been involved in his other criminal activities?"

Shelby supposed she should have seen that one coming, but she hadn't. More fool she. Was Derek looking for a scapegoat if he couldn't get Christopher? Would she provide the warm body in her brother's stead? Derek had political aspirations after all.

She was bitter and angry. She felt railroaded. Worse though, she felt pain that threatened to overwhelm her. Derek hadn't come here on any pretense of friendship. She'd known all along he would be doing his job. But then so was Mitch.

A rush of tears blurred her vision. She got to her feet, angry with herself for showing any weakness in front of Mitch. Her legs wobbled but she managed to step away from the table and remain upright.

From behind her, Mitch reached out and gently clasped her arm. "Shelby?"

"I'm going to the washroom." She broke his hold and bolted for the stairs.

* * *

Mitch watched her run up the steps. Tears had drenched her eyes yet she'd made it past him before they fell and he'd see how hurt she was. He didn't need a mind reader to know she felt betrayed. By him. Mitch swung toward Derek. "What the fuck was that?"

Derek exhaled deeply. "I took it as easy on her as I could. But, Mitch, we didn't come here for a tea party."

Mitch glared at Derek. "You were out of line."

"I'm just trying to get this guy, same as you."

"Shelby's work for her brother began and ended with my investigation."

"Look." Derek held up a hand. "If she's dealt with her brother in this way before, she may know something we can use against him."

"She doesn't know anything more than she's already told you." Mitch had his own suspicions and doubts about her, but he'd be damned before he'd listen to anyone else doubt her. "I won't stand by and let you grill her."

"Okay. Okay." Derek shook his head. "You're right. I went over the top. I'll apologize to Shelby." He blew out a deep breath. "I wanted to find out if Shelby had any more skeletons in her closet."

"That has nothing to do with this investigation and don't give me any more bullshit about Shelby lending insight into her brother's business." Mitch narrowed his eyes at Derek. "What's really going on here?"

Derek scratched his jaw and twisted his lips. "I had to get that out."

"No, you didn't. Shelby isn't the one going to trial. Rossington is." Mitch pointed a finger at Derek. "If you're looking to also pin something on her, I'm not going to let you hang her out to dry."

"That's not what I'm doing." Derek rubbed a hand back through his hair. "The Feds want to talk to her. You know Agent Polleck is going to bring that up."

"And you wanted to make sure he didn't find anything you hadn't." Mitch clenched his jaw. "Covering your ass, Derek?" Mitch's tone dripped with sarcasm. "You can tell Polleck I said he can go to hell. Shelby has nothing to say to him."

"It's only a matter of time before he insists."

"I haven't asked for the Bureau's help. He has no jurisdiction here." But Rossington's crimes weren't restricted to Blake County and organized crime was a federal matter. Derek was right, eventually, the FBI would come calling.

Mitch turned away from Derek and started toward the stairs.

"Mitch—"

He turned back to face Derek. "If you want to speak with Shelby again, it will be with her lawyer present. This interview is over."

CHAPTER ELEVEN

Shelby bent over the sink in the church restroom and cupped her hands beneath the flow of cool water. Her hands were shaking and the water slid through her fingers. Giving up, she took a paper towel from the dispenser, soaked that and pressed it to her face instead.

She needed to put herself back together before she returned to answer more of Derek's questions. She needed to be at full capacity to keep up her guard. Derek was looking to trip her up, to get her to admit to something. Her fingers tightened on the towel. She didn't know anything about Christopher's foul business. She may be the only one who believed that. Mitch certainly didn't.

What did he think she was hiding? What could be worse than what she'd already confessed?

"Shelby."

Mitch's voice penetrated the closed door. Clearly, her time was up.

"I'll be out in a minute," she said.

"Are you all right?"

Was he joking? How could she be all right? "I'll be out in a minute," she repeated. "You and Derek are just going to have to wait." Her tone was laced with bitterness and sadness. She regretted that. She'd shown Mitch enough weakness tonight.

"The interview is over," Mitch said.

Shelby's stomach fluttered. Over?

"Shelby?"

She dropped the towel into the waste basket then went to the door and opened it.

Mitch was standing right outside beneath the light from a ceiling fixture. His eyes were dark with anger and his face was hard as stone. Shelby didn't know why he would be angry and didn't care at this moment. While she was glad to be spared further questions, she had to know why she'd been spared. In her experience a reprieve didn't come without a cost.

"Why did Derek end this?" she asked.

"He didn't. I did."

"Why would you do that? This is what you wanted."

Mitch's brows lowered and his gaze became intent on her. "I didn't like the direction Derek was taking. And, for the record, I didn't know he was going to take that line with you. I never agreed to that. I would never have agreed to that. I'm sorry I put you through this. More sorry than you'll ever know." He reached out and cupped her face. "I don't want you to worry that Derek is going to be looking to pin anything on you. That isn't going to happen. I won't let that happen."

His eyes blazed with the strength of his conviction.

Why the change of heart? Though, he had said he'd never intended for the questioning to take the turn it had.

"Are you ready to go?" Mitch asked.

"More than."

He was still holding her face. He brushed his thumb down her cheek once, then lowered his hand. His voice gentle, he said, "Let's get out of here."

Shelby could feel his touch even after he'd removed his hand. She'd missed it. Missed him. *Don't go there.* She closed her eyes and when she reopened them Mitch was at the front door, holding it open for her. She brushed by him and led the way back to his SUV.

Dawn was still about forty-five minutes away. She leaned her head against the seat, feeling wrung out, and looked out at the dark night as they left the church behind. They were a good distance from any main roads and the only traffic they encountered was a bread truck.

"I can't take you back to the clinic," Mitch said. "We need to secure you and I need to see my dad and Ellen. Make arrangements for their safety as well until Rossington is in custody."

Shelby closed her eyes. Yes, of course. Christopher was still at large. Hurting Ed and Ellen, to strike out at Mitch, wasn't beneath him. Mitch's father and step-mother needed to be secured. She'd brought this to them. It was her fault their lives were in danger from Christopher now.

Mitch pulled out his cell phone and told his father they were on their way. Dawn was breaking when they arrived at the elder Turner house. Mitch led her to the back, to the door that opened into the kitchen. She gazed into the room through the small window in the door. Ellen was at the stove, flipping sizzling yokes. An apron hung on her thin frame. She threw her head back, sending waves of silver hair off her face, and laughed at something Ed must have said. He was seated at the laminate table, watching her with his heart in his eyes. Shelby watched them, saving the moment to memory, before Mitch pushed the door open.

She didn't want to go inside with him. Didn't want to be told she was unwelcome or made to feel it once they'd heard what Mitch had to tell them. She couldn't blame them if they told her to leave.

She hung back on the threshold. "I can wait here."

"I'm not leaving you alone."

Mitch placed his hand at the small of her back and Shelby went inside ahead of him. The kitchen was small in keeping with the rest of the house. The cabinetry and flooring had dulled and scuffed from years of toddler and adolescent hands and feet on them. The appliances looked original to the old house. Shelby loved this kitchen. It was a testament to all the love this family shared.

The scents of bacon, ham, and potatoes frying, along with the aroma of strong coffee filled the air. At their entrance, Ellen set the spatula on the counter and turned to them. Her hands flew to her cheeks and she laughed in obvious delight. Leaning heavily on a thick, pronged cane, and forgoing the wheel chair beside him, Ed greeted them at the door. A shoulder squeeze for Mitch, and his typical bear hug for Shelby. The bullet had left Ed with permanent damage to his back and even this short distance should have been covered in the wheelchair. Regardless of his discomfort, he enveloped Shelby. She felt like a thief, stealing this affection from him under false pretenses. Still she didn't pull away but clung to him, returning his embrace for all she was worth.

When Ed finally released her, he raised one thick, white brow then asked, "What's up that you're both here at the crack of dawn?"

"I've made breakfast," Ellen said. "Let's catch up while we eat."

Rising on tiptoe, Ellen placed one hand on Mitch's face and gave him a kiss on the cheek. Mitch wrapped an arm around her in an affectionate hug. She gave Shelby the same warm attention then clasped one of Shelby's hands and one of Mitch's and led them both to the table, already set for four.

While the meal Ellen had prepared was left to grow cold, Mitch laid it out for them, quick and neat. But he didn't tell them she'd lied to him. He'd spared her their judgment. Why? Shelby couldn't explain it since he'd judged her himself.

Ellen's and Ed's faces reflected shock and disbelief, particularly at learning that the threat came from Shelby's brother. Mitch hadn't told them of her lies to him, but they still had plenty to rightfully condemn her for. Coward that she was, Shelby looked away from them.

Mitch regarded his father and Ellen. "I need you both to get out of here for awhile. I've arranged for you to go to a safe house until Rossington is in custody. Two of my men are on their way now to take you there. You'll need to pack a few things quickly."

Ellen's hand went to her throat where she fingered a heart-shaped locket that Shelby knew held boyhood pictures of Mitch and his brother. She wasn't the mother of Ed's children, but Ellen couldn't love them more.

"You think this Rossington fellow will make some kind of grab for us, Mitch?" Ellen asked.

Mitch reached out and covered Ellen's hand with his. He brought it to his lips and kissed the back of it. "I'm not taking the chance. Please, Ellen, pack some things for you and Dad now."

Ellen's brows drew tight. She looked to Ed, who sat tight-lipped and pale-faced, then back to Mitch. Mitch nodded and released her hand. Ellen rose slowly to her feet then left the kitchen.

Shelby watched her go. Mitch's father and Ellen had welcomed her, treating her like their own beloved child. Ed called her "daughter" and had invited her to call him "Dad". She wanted to so badly. This man was a true father, so unlike the man who'd sired her. Despite her deep longing, she'd never called him that. Given the deception she'd perpetuated on them all, it would be a mockery. She loved these people so much. That she'd brought this to them, put them in danger, felt like a dagger piercing her heart. She didn't know how she'd live with herself if they were harmed because of her. She closed her eyes hard enough to hurt. Telling herself that Christopher had left her no choice but to follow his orders didn't assuage her guilt or her pain.

Ed shook his head from side to side like an enraged bull. One hand fisted on the table. "We'll go with your people, son. The last thing I want is for you to be worried about us. But what about the two of you?" He looked from Mitch to Shelby, then back to Mitch.

Shelby couldn't believe he'd asked after her well-being.

"I'll be securing Shelby as well," Mitch said. His cell phone rang and he got up from the table to take the call.

Shelby swallowed tears that clogged her throat and shoring up her courage, addressed Ed. "I'm so sorry I brought this to you." Her voice broke. "I'm so sorry."

Mitch's father struggled to his feet, teetering before he gained his balance. Shelby wanted to spring up from her chair and help him, but didn't think he'd want assistance from her. Ed rounded the table to her. He bent with obvious difficulty and put his arms around her, squeezing her against him. His affection, in the face of what she'd brought to them, brought more tears to her eyes.

"Your daughter is safe and we're all going to be too," Ed said, his voice strangely thick.

Shelby held onto him and prayed that he was right.

The sound of voices behind her drew her

attention. Ed gripped the table for support and turned to the door as she did. Mitch's officers had arrived. He must have briefed the two men, Rolando and Quinn, earlier because once he'd introduced them, they whisked Ed and Ellen out of the house on their way to the safe location Mitch had designated.

Mitch led Shelby out a few moments later. In Mitch's SUV, Shelby looked out of the passenger side window but noticed little. Her emotions were frayed. Those moments with Ed in the kitchen had remained with her. Ed had reassured her, comforted her when she was the reason he'd been forced to leave his home when it was barely daylight, his life uprooted.

Mitch had said to Ed that he'd be securing her as well. Where were they going? Mitch had a cabin in a remote section of the Adirondack Mountains. She'd never been there because Gage had been using it for most of the time she'd been with Mitch. Were they going there?

Was Mitch deliberately not telling her where he was taking her? Did he still think she would go running to her brother, or was this how he operated on an investigation, on all investigations? She knew first-hand what a tight rein he'd kept on information pertaining to this one.

Did it matter where the safe house was? Not really. She was in a holding state for the next while. Watching. Waiting until Christopher was in custody and she could offer testimony against him, and then again until he was convicted and incarcerated. Could she believe that Christopher was really going to be put away? Did she dare to hope?

"I don't want to stop for breakfast." Mitch's voice brought her out of her thoughts. "I'd rather we waited until we arrived and ate then. It's not far now. Can you wait?"

"I'm fine."

She'd noticed Mitch's glance lift to his rearview mirror while they'd been driving, checking if they were being followed, no doubt. Nothing in his expression or in his driving had altered which she took as a sign that all was well.

A short while later, Mitch pulled into a run-down area that had once been industrial but now looked long abandoned. A couple of dilapidated warehouses stood. The signs that bore the names of the companies the warehouses belonged to had long since faded, the paint chipped and cracked so Shelby couldn't make them out. What were they doing here?

Before she could ask him that question, the door to the warehouse rolled up and Mitch drove inside.

"We're staying here," Mitch said.

"This is the safe house?"

"One of them, yeah." Mitch parked his vehicle beside a tan sedan. "I packed some things for you from what you left at my house."

"Thank you."

He took two suitcases from the rear of the vehicle. An elevator took them to a loft that had been made into an apartment. Two apartments, actually, she saw when they stepped into a long corridor. A door was open and two men joined them in the hall.

"Shelby, meet Detectives Church and Morales."

"How do, ma'am," Church said. He was a tall fair-haired man who spoke in a slow, southern drawl.

Morales nodded at Shelby. He was large, as large as Mitch, with dark hair and skin.

"Any trouble?" Mitch asked.

"Nothin' Chief," Church said.

Mitch turned to Shelby. "Let's get you settled."

The apartment wasn't large, but it did have two bedrooms. A half-wall separated a kitchen from a living room. Shelby looked around but couldn't find a phone. Mitch had taken her cell phone the day he'd learned of her association with Christopher and had yet to return it.

"I'd like to speak with Sara," Shelby said.

Mitch set the suitcases down in the living room and unclipped his phone from his belt. After a brief exchange with Zach, where Mitch received a status report, he handed the phone to Shelby. Sara's tiny voice came on the line.

"Mama."

Tears filled Shelby's eyes. She swallowed them back and smiled. "Hi, sweetie."

"Peekaboo, Mama." Sara giggled.

Sara went on about Doc Brock's "puple 'phant" that Shelby took to mean "purple elephant." Brock had a series of books that Shelby had been reading to Sara about the adventures of a purple elephant. Shelby just listened, enjoying the joy in her child's voice. After a few minutes, Sara yawned loudly.

"Sleepy, Mama."

Shelby had to clear her throat again before she could respond. Though it was morning, she said, "Night, night Sara."

Zach came on the line. "It's lights out for Sara. If there's nothing else?" Zach's tone was brisk.

"No," Shelby said. "Nothing else."

Zach disconnected. He remained distant and abrupt. That wasn't likely to change. Despite his disillusionment with her, though, she had no doubt he guarded Sara with his life and Shelby was grateful.

More than Sara's medical needs were being met by Brock, Laurel, their staff, by Mitch's officers, and by Zach. Shelby couldn't measure her gratitude, yet her cheeks heated with a rush of anger. She slapped the phone in Mitch's palm.

He replaced the phone on his belt, keeping his eyes on her. "You okay?"

When she didn't respond, Mitch spoke again. "Sara's okay and she's going to stay that way."

"As long as she remains at Brock's."

Mitch nodded slowly. "For now, yeah."

"Christopher's always one step ahead."

"Not this time." Mitch tipped her chin up so she was looking into his eyes. "What's this about?"

She tried to turn her head and avert her gaze, but just as he'd done at the church, Mitch held her in place. "I've spent more time away from my child than with her because of Christopher."

Mitch frowned. "Tell me."

"It's a wonder my daughter knows me at all. Sara and I have never lived in one place for any length of time. We don't even share the same last name. I haven't ever been able to acknowledge my child." Shelby told Mitch of constantly being on the move and the precautions she'd taken to keep Sara hidden. "We've never lived together for more than a day or two and the last time we did, Christopher came and took her."

Mitch's lips pulled tight forming two white slashes. "I will take that bastard out."

So far, her brother had been invincible. He'd always been invincible. And now Mitch's family was at risk. "I'm sorry, Mitch. Your dad and Ellen shouldn't be involved in this." Shelby fisted her hands in impotent anger and frustration. "I should have found a way out of spying on you for Christopher and still kept Sara safe. If I hadn't brought her home that last night ..." She drew a shaky breath. "I'm so, so sorry." It all was too much and came crashing down on her. Tears slid down her cheeks before she even realized she was crying.

Mitch drew her against him and wrapped his arms around her. "Your brother must have been watching you, biding his time for an opportunity to take Sara. You did everything possible to keep her safe. There wasn't anything more you could do. I can't stand thinking of how you've lived on the run. That life is over for you, I promise you. This is the last time you'll have to be separated from your daughter."

* * *

Mitch's words had not been idle. It was a vow,

he'd just made to Shelby. She was clinging to him, trembling in his arms, her strength depleted, her spirit crushed. He couldn't stand to see her laid so low. Every muscle in his body tensed with rage. If Rossington deserved to fry for nothing else, he deserved to fry for this.

Mitch tightened his hold around her. His doubts about her innocence ended. If anything or anyone in this world tried to hurt her again, they would have to go through him. God help Rossington if he tried to take her from him.

A knock at the door had Mitch swinging around, braced for a fight. Church's voice came through the door.

"Chief?" Church's voice was tense. "We got trouble."

CHAPTER TWELVE

Mitch still had one arm around Shelby and kept it there, taking her with him to the door. He threw it open to admit Church. "What is it?"

"Dispatch put a call through to our secure line. The FBI guy assigned to this area, Polleck. He wants to know our location."

Mitch didn't ask why Polleck wanted to know where they were. He knew the answer— Shelby. His blood heated with anger. "And?"

Church shook his head quickly. "I didn't give it to him, of course. He's holding for you."

With Shelby by his side, Mitch went to take the call. The room they'd set up as a command post with its various monitors, communication devices, and weaponry was empty. Morales was working night surveillance while Church covered the day, and Morales was presumably fast asleep.

Mitch picked up the phone. "Polleck."

"I got your message from Derek."

"Glad to hear it." Mitch's voice was hard.

"That's why I sent it."

Polleck's teeth clacked together in obvious anger. "You can't just disappear with Rossington's sister. We need to talk with her."

"Shelby Grant has nothing to say to you. Get that." Shelby sucked in a breath and stiffened in his arms. Mitch tightened his hold on her.

Polleck softened his tone. "Mitch, I don't need to tell you how badly we want Christopher Rossington. Hell, you must want him as well after that car bomb that killed three of your men."

Yeah, he wanted Rossington. Mitch's jaw tightened. "Hear me, Polleck, Shelby is not your ticket to Rossington. She doesn't know anything more than she's already told us."

"I know this is personal for you, Mitch. I know you're engaged to marry Dr. Grant. Bring her to me. I'm not going to hurt her. I'm going to protect her, same as you."

Mitch's voice lowered, became deadly. "Let's get this straight. Shelby stays with me."

Polleck's voice sharpened. "What about you, Chief? Your fiancée is the sister of a crime boss whose been on our radar for years. Don't think I'm not taking a long look at you now."

"You threatening me, Polleck?" Mitch's tone dripped acid. "You don't know me at all if you think that's going to make me roll over and play dead. You want to look at me? Go for it."

"I'm going to take over your investigation." Polleck's voice quavered with anger. "Force you to hand her over."

Mitch's fury reached boiling point. "I'm not handing my investigation over to you. You're not getting shit from me. And I'm sure as fuck not going to give you Shelby." The words came out as a snarl. "This is the last time I'm going to tell you. Shelby stays with me."

He disconnected, then threw the phone onto the desk. He turned to Church. "When Morales relieves you, tell him I want to see him." Mitch gave Church a hard look. "Polleck gets nothing from us. Got that?"

Church nodded. "Yes, sir."

Shelby had paled. Damn Polleck. Mitch led her back to the apartment they were using. Inside, before Mitch could address her fear, Shelby turned to him.

She swallowed several times, then said, "What does the FBI want with me? I gave a statement to the DA. Won't that suffice?"

Mitch's instinct was to shield her, but she deserved to know the truth. "Polleck, the FBI field agent, doesn't want a copy of your statement. He wants me to hand you over to him."

Shelby shivered. "That's why you told him I'm staying with you?"

"Yeah."

"Can Polleck force me to go with him? And if he does, what about Sara? Can he take her too?"

Shelby's voice had risen, become strident. Mitch took her hands in his. "I'm not going to let that happen."

"Which means you'll have a fight on your hands to keep me with you. It would be so much easier for you to turn me over to the FBI. You'd be rid of me and all the trouble I've brought to you." She uttered the words in a whisper.

Her breath quickened. Goose bumps sprang on her arms where the elbow-length sleeves on her blouse didn't cover. Mitch framed her face between his palms, forcing her to look directly at him. "You're not going anywhere. Trust me."

"Does this mean you now trust me?" She reached up to where his hands still held her face and curled her fingers around his wrists. "Mitch, do you believe me about Christopher?"

Mitch could feel the slight tremble in her hands. Her eyes were wide, pleading. His heart did a slow roll. He no longer doubted her. It was time he told her that. "I believe you."

He held her gaze and eyes open, covered her mouth with his. Everything in him shouted: Mine. He lowered his hands from her face, and wrapped his arms around her, crushing her against him.

Shelby kissed him with the same intensity, then moved slightly so she could look at him and still touch her lips to his. "Thank you for believing me. I hated that you didn't believe me." She closed her eyes for an instant. "Couldn't believe me."

When her eyes opened again, he stared into them. "Not believing you, not trusting you was killing me."

She made a small mewling sound as if she were in pain. "I swear you'll never have reason to doubt me again."

He raised a hand and cradled her nape. "I want to touch you." He kissed her, a soft glancing of his lips against hers. "I need to touch you."

Her mouth trembled against his. "I need that,

ed her into his mouth. Shelby gasped and made another soft sound of desire that sent a rush of blood to his arousal and ratcheted up his already raging lust.

He shed his own clothing, then slid down her body and moved between her thighs. He spread her gently and licked her. Shelby came off the bed. She grasped his head to hold him in place, but he wasn't going anywhere. He kept up a steady rhythm. Shelby writhed. Her head thrashed on the pillow. Mitch clasped her legs to hold her in place.

He couldn't get enough of her and yet his muscles were taut as bowstrings with the effort of containing his release. He closed his eyes to pull himself back from the edge but his other senses took over. Beneath his hands and his mouth, he could feel her quivering with desire. His every breath was filled with her feminine scent. When she gasped his name, her voice breathy with passion, Mitch couldn't hold out any longer. As

159

Shelby came apart in his arms, he entered her, one hard fast, thrust. Gritting his teeth, he pulled back slowly. She clamped tight around him and he lost it, shouting out his own release.

Mitch caught himself before he collapsed on top of her. They were still joined and he slowly reversed their positions, so she lay atop him, without separating. The sensations from their lovemaking hadn't subsided but as incredible as those feelings were, there was more to why he remained joined to her in this way. His hold on her body was possessive. This woman was his.

He could feel her heart pounding and feel her soft breath against his neck. He brought one arm to the back of her hair and cradled her head against him, loving the feel of her in his arms. Shelby reached out to his other hand and linked their fingers.

For security, there were no windows in any of the rooms. Mitch hadn't taken time to switch on a light but the bedroom was small and light from the hall was sufficient to make out a dark wood dresser, one nightstand, the double bed they were on, and Shelby, soft and sated.

He sifted his fingers through her hair. She sighed. He smiled. She loved when he stroked her hair.

"If you do that, I'm going to fall asleep," she said.

Her voice was already thickening. "You've been awake for more than twenty four hours, honey. You're long overdue. Go ahead and sleep."

"Not yet. I don't want to sleep yet."

She raised her head and looked at him. Her hair was tousled from their lovemaking and from his fingers. Her cheeks were flushed. Her lips swollen from his kisses. He brushed the back of his finger against her full bottom lip. "You are so incredibly beautiful."

He lifted her slightly so he could kiss her. He'd intended a soft, tender caress of her lips as a prelude to sleep, but the instant he touched her, that all changed and he thickened and hardened inside her. He moved them again and was back above her. That slight friction had him throbbing. "God, Shelby, I want you again." His jaw pulled tight.

She reached up and brushed the sweat-damp hair from his brow. "I'm right here," she said gently.

Her sweetness almost finished him and he didn't want that. He placed his brow against hers and took a panting breath. "This is going to go too fast if we stay the way we are." Gritting his teeth he withdrew from her. He vaulted off the bed then scooped her up into his arms. Shelby grabbed his neck and laughed. He laughed with her as he carried her to the shower.

He set her carefully on her feet on the white tile. The glass doors were open. He gave the taps a twist. The walk from the bed had done nothing to cool him down. He was burning for her. His erection as hard as granite. What he needed to make this last was cold water, but he wasn't going to put Shelby into a cold tub.

When he had the water warm enough, he clasped her around the waist and stepped beneath the hot spray with her. He set her back against the tile, then reached out to close the shower doors.

Water pearled on her skin. Mitch groaned and put his lips to the fine drops on her brow, following their trail down her body. He knew all of the spots that drove her insane with need and he was going to reacquaint himself with every one of them.

He kissed the pulse point in her neck then sucked it gently into his mouth. Beneath his lips, her pulse began to race. She leaned her head back against the tile and slid down the wall a bit as if her legs would no longer fully support her. He caught her on the descent and wrapped his arm tight around her.

He slid his lips along the curve of her shoulder, dipping his tongue into the small hollow of her collar bone. Shelby's teeth bit into her lower lip. He flicked his thumb across one nipple, watched it pucker. Her eyes glazed and Mitch's erection kicked and swelled more. Before he could take her breast into his mouth, Shelby gave him a nudge.

"I have to touch you," she said. "Let me touch you."

Breathing hard, she dropped to her knees. Wrapping both hands around him, she took him into her mouth. Mitch shook. His blood pounded. He squeezed his eyes shut and bit down on his teeth as she stimulated his every nerve ending with long slow laps of her tongue. When he knew he couldn't take anymore, he eased her back.

"Baby, enough." He hooked her beneath the arms and lifted her, ending her sweet torment.

"Wrap your arms around my neck." His voice was hoarse and urgent.

When she complied, he braced her against the tile. Beneath the pounding spray of the water, he lowered her onto himself. Slowly, he filled her, inch by inch until all of him was inside her. He could go no deeper and just as slowly as he'd entered her, he lifted her off him again.

She dug her nails into his back. "Mitch … now."

Her urgent plea snapped his control. He drove into her harder, faster. He found her mouth with his and as she tightened around him he swallowed her cry of release. He shuddered and shouted out his own completion.

Shelby's head fell onto his neck as if she were unable to support it any longer. He held her against him as their breathing normalized and then he sought her mouth once again and pressed a tender kiss to her lips. Her arms were already around his neck. He swept her up and stepped out of the shower. Towels? Likely in the cupboard beneath the sink. He sat her on the vanity and got one then carefully dried her with it. After, he dried himself, then lifted her into his arms again.

Back in the bedroom, he set her down on the mattress then joined her on the bed. His brows drew together and he leaned over her. He took her hand and pressed a kiss to her palm.

Tears shimmered in her eyes.

He kissed her again long and slow, then drew the bedcovers over them. She gave him a sleepy smile. Her eyelids drooped as she burrowed into his side.

Mitch watched her sleep. His woman. He felt a return of the contentment he'd only known with her. He smoothed a lock of hair that fell across her cheek then tenderly caressed her skin. He was tempted to move his hand lower, to the curve of her gorgeous bottom, but held back, not wanting to risk waking her.

She was safe here in this apartment. He'd made sure of that. He'd make sure she was safe everywhere. Rossington would not touch her. Mitch's mouth firmed. Not while he was still breathing. It was time he drew that bastard out.

* * *

Shelby woke to the scents of bacon and eggs frying. Her stomach rumbled. She hadn't thought about food in hours but now she was definitely thinking about it. Mitch must have food on the brain as well since he'd left the bed. A glance at the glowing numbers on the bedside clock told her it was after eight p.m. They'd slept the day away.

It was no wonder they were both hungry after the morning they'd had. She could feel the smile spread across her lips. She was wonderfully lethargic and blissfully aware of parts of her body where Mitch had focused their lovemaking.

She hadn't expected to be like this with Mitch ever again. It felt like a miracle that she was. She glanced at her hand where she still wore his ring. In all that had happened, she'd never given it back to him. She'd accepted it under false pretenses, never expecting she'd have a life with him. Naive to hope now that he would want to marry her. That he could ever want that again. Could ever feel that depth of love for her again. Her heart gave a hard thud but she wouldn't spoil this moment by thinking beyond it. He was with her now and for now, it was enough.

Mitch's shirt was hanging off the end of the bed. It still held his scent. She breathed deeply of it, loving the smell of him, before slipping it on. The shirt fell to her knees. She buttoned it then wrapped the sleeves back several inches until her hands were visible. Barefoot, she padded out to the kitchen.

Mitch stood at the stove. His hair was damp from the shower. As she neared she could smell soap and shampoo. He wore jeans and a T-shirt that couldn't mask the muscles in his upper body. He hadn't shaved and the stubble that darkened his jaw only made him sexier. She stared for a moment, appreciating the sight of him.

He looked up from the pan of scrambled eggs. "Since we never got around to breakfast, I thought we'd have it now."

She smiled. "Sounds great."

He stretched out an arm in invitation. She went to him and leaned up to accept his kiss. Unhurried, he drew it out, sliding his tongue along her lips before delving inside her mouth. She met his tongue with hers caress for caress. When he drew back his breath wasn't as steady as it had been. Neither was hers. It felt wonderful.

"I borrowed your shirt," she said. "Hope you don't mind."

Mitch's gaze heated. "That shirt never looked

that good on me."

She delighted in their easy banter. "I wouldn't say that." She kissed him again then went to the coffee pot where Mitch had set out two white mugs.

He glanced back at her over his shoulder. "Chamomile tea's in the cupboard above the sink."

Shelby had expected to drink coffee. She was surprised and so touched that he'd checked if there was tea for her. Ninny. She was being a ninny to make so much out of a few bags of tea, but the happiness she felt at his thoughtfulness didn't go away.

"Where did all this come from?" She gestured to the food as she put the kettle on to boil.

"Church and Morales came out to get the place ready before we got here."

"What about them? Don't Detectives Church and Morales want to eat?"

"They have their own set up. They're fine."

A few moments later, the kettle whistled. Shelby made tea and they filled plates and took them to the small kitchen table. It was a testament to how hungry they both were that they ate in silence.

When Shelby couldn't eat another bite, she rose from her seat. "You cooked. I'll clean up."

Mitch grinned. "I'll get the broom."

"You can stay right where you are." She held up a hand and laughed. "No dishes will be broken today."

It was a running joke between them. She'd broken several glasses and plates at Mitch's while helping him clean up after meals.

"Growing up, I don't think you did a lot of dishes." Mitch asked the question softly.

Shelby's laughter died. "No. My father employed a full staff."

"You never mentioned your mother."

Shelby's hand tightened on her napkin. "She died soon after I graduated high school."

"Tell me about her."

Shelby had no reason not to tell him. "It was difficult to be close with my mother. What she felt for my father went beyond love, she worshiped him. No matter how many times he hurt her, physically or emotionally with his verbal abuse and with his affairs. No matter how bad it got, her feelings never changed. The only time she ever struck me was when I spoke out against him.

"She wanted to give him what he wanted most in this world—more sons. Apparently after she gave birth to me—a girl—he became so enraged at her that he beat her almost to death. He would never believe his biology determined that I was born female." Shelby's lips twisted bitterly. "My mother wasn't able to conceive again after that. She wouldn't accept the doctor's diagnosis and spent years praying for a miracle and ingesting any alleged cure she could find. When she went into menopause, she knew she'd run out of time to have more children. She filled her bathtub with water and drowned herself. I found her. I went to look for her when she didn't come down for breakfast." Tears gathered and burned Shelby's throat and eyes. "My father was pure evil." She shuddered. "Whatever your Intel told you about him, it wasn't enough."

Mitch rose from his seat and took the few steps separating them. He took her into his arms. One hand held the back of her head pressed to his chest while the other arm wound around her. "I'm sorry, sweetheart." He kissed her hair.

Tears fell onto her cheeks and soaked into his shirt. Mitch held her tighter. She took the comfort he offered, something she'd never been given at the time her mother died by anyone, least of all her father and brother.

"I've never spoken of that day to anyone," she said quietly.

Mitch rested his chin on top of her head. "I can't stand thinking of you going through that. Of what you've endured from your father and brother." Mitch's voice was harsh with fury.

Shelby pressed closer to him and her voice muffled against his chest. "My father was already dead when I had Sara. So unfair that after all the pain he'd caused he should die peacefully in his sleep." She spat out the words. "Christopher learned from the master and he will make Sara's life the hell mine is. I was selfish to bring a child into my world."

Mitch stiffened as if hesitating then said. "It takes two to make a child."

She raised her head from his chest and looked up at him. "I met Paul, Sara's father, at a conference, like I told you. I hadn't been with anyone in a very long time. He was fun, carefree, and spontaneous, three things I wasn't. Paul and I were together for the length of the conference and I got pregnant." She shook her head. "I was taking precautions. I don't know how that happened. He didn't want to get married and he certainly didn't want to be a father. That suited me. I never told him where I came from or the danger he would be in if he stayed with me."

She clutched Mitch's arm. "I'd always avoided relationships because of what my father and brother could do to a man I became seriously involved with. When I found out I was pregnant, I should not have gone ahead with the pregnancy." She lowered her gaze. "But I couldn't end that precious life. I told myself I'd give her up to a good, loving home when she was born, but when the time came I couldn't do that." She lifted her eyes to Mitch once more. "When I looked at Sara for the first time, I loved her so much. I wanted her so much. I was ready to do anything I had to, to keep her."

Mitch wiped the tears trailing down her cheeks with his thumbs. "You wanted your daughter. That's nothing to blame yourself for. Your brother is the cause of all this and I swear he will never hurt you again." Mitch's eyes blazed. "You're not fighting him by yourself this time. This time to get to you, he'll have to go through me."

Shelby pressed her face against his chest again and clung to him. He could never know what his words meant to her. For the first time in her life, she didn't feel alone.

Sara was safe. Ed and Ellen were safe. Shelby herself was safe and she let herself believe that Christopher was not all powerful and he would finally be out of her life forever.

Mitch's cell phone rang. He kissed her temple and slowly loosened his hold while he unclipped his phone. "I need to take this." He put the phone to his ear. "Turner." He listened to his caller for some time, then said. "Good. Let's get this done." He ended the call and focused on Shelby. "I need to talk to you—"

A knock on the door interrupted him. "Chief? Church said you want to talk to me?"

Morales. Shelby recognized his voice.

"I'll be right there," Mitch called out to Morales. Mitch rubbed his hands up and down Shelby's arms. "Give me a few minutes, baby, then we'll talk."

His serious expression had her stomach knotting. "Mitch?"

"When I get back."

He kissed her again then left the apartment.

CHAPTER THIRTEEN

Mitch had not known the history leading up to Elizabeth Rossington's death or that she'd ended her own life. Rossington must have had that covered up.

Mitch could only imagine the horror Shelby had suffered finding her mother dead. One more horror in a life of nothing but. It was a wonder she'd survived at all. Mitch didn't want to think about what her childhood and subsequent years living with her father and brother had been like, but of course, he did.

"Chief?"

They'd reached the command room. Mitch brought himself back to the reason he wanted to speak with Morales then told his detective of Polleck's interest in Shelby and their stance on it.

Morales nodded. "Polleck won't get anything from us, sir."

Mitch nodded. "Anything I need to know about?"

"Church said it was quiet all day." Morales scratched his chin. "We did have a little disturbance right before I came to see you."

"Oh?"

"Two kids with piece of shit cars looking to drag."

Mitch's brows lowered. The last thing he needed was a bunch of kids deciding this deserted area would be the perfect spot to hold a drag race. "Where are they now?"

"Gone. Turns out these two vehicles had nothing under the hoods. The whole thing was over before it got started and the kids cleared out."

That's what Mitch wanted to hear. "We're taking a new direction with Rossington. Get Church. I need to go over a few things with you both now."

* * *

Mitch finished briefing his men, then returned to Shelby. She must have been listening for his return because as soon as he reached the door, she opened it. She'd changed out of his shirt and into jeans and a flowing blouse.

"What's going on?" she asked.

Mitch closed the apartment door then put his arm around her shoulders and led her to the couch. While she perched on the end of it, he sat on the sturdy chest-style coffee table opposite her.

He took her hand loosely in his. "I'm going to be leaving for a while."

"Where are we going?"

"You're not going anywhere, honey. You'll be staying here with Morales and Church. I just briefed them. I'm the only one leaving."

"Why?"

"You'll be safe here. I wouldn't leave you if I weren't certain of that."

"That's not what I mean. I know you'll keep me safe. Where are you going? Have you caught Christopher?"

Mitch let out a frustrated grunt. "No. It's time we smoked him out."

Shelby's brows drew together and she bit into her lower lip. "How?"

"We're going to show ourselves."

"But you just said I'm not leaving?"

"You're not. I am. One of my female detectives will pose as you. We'll use her as bait to draw Rossington out."

"He won't be fooled."

"We'll make sure to provide only glimpses of her and not a full view."

Shelby shook her head. "You need to use me, then there'd be no concern about fooling him."

Mitch's mouth went tight. "Not an option."

Two spots of red appeared on Shelby's pale cheeks. Her voice vibrated with anger. "You think you know him, but you don't. He won't be drawn out by a decoy. You need to take me with you. He'll want revenge on me for betraying him to you. He'll come out of wherever he's hiding to get to me."

Mitch leaned forward and gave her the full force of his stare. "Are you so willing to sacrifice yourself? Because if you are, I'm not." His voice was fierce.

"That's not what I'm doing. Am I afraid of revealing myself to Christopher? I'd be a fool not to be." She shivered, but didn't back down. "I want a life, Mitch. I'll never have that until Christopher is put away."

"You'll have your life. I swear it." His face tightened with the rage he was feeling at Rossington.

Shelby squeezed his hand. Hers was trembling. "Christopher won't give you many chances to get to him. This may be your only chance. You're saying it's a matter of my safety, but you're going to protect your decoy from him. You know you can protect me. I know you can protect me."

He understood her desperation to be rid of her bastard brother, but he would get this done without her. With each operation there was an element of risk no matter how well planned or manned. He would not risk her. He eyed her. "Yeah, I can and I will protect you. The best way for me to do that is to keep you here."

Mitch held her gaze. There was no give in him on this. She must have seen that and realized there was no point in arguing this further with him.

"When are you leaving?" she asked softly.

"Shortly."

"That soon?" Shelby reached up and touched his injured brow gently, then leaned forward until her body was against his. "Be careful."

Mitch put his arms around her, so her head was beneath his jaw. "Count on it."

She seemed reluctant to move out of his arms and that suited him just fine. There was no place he'd rather have her. He tilted her face up and was about to kiss her when Morales's voice reached them through the closed front door.

"Chief? Detective Rolando is holding for your folks on the secure line."

Mitch got to his feet, taking Shelby with him. When they reached the command room, Morales didn't enter with them but continued down the hall.

Mitch picked up the receiver. "Turner."

"Chief? Rolando here. Just a second and I'll put Mrs. Turner on."

Mitch heard the phone being passed then Ellen's voice. "Mitch?"

"Yes, Ellen, I'm here."

"We've been missing you and Shelby. We checked with Detective Rolando and he said it was all right to call you. I hope I'm not taking you away from anything."

"Not at all."

"How are you and Shelby?"

Mitch's gaze went to Shelby. "We're fine."

Shelby put her ear close to his so she could hear Ellen's side of the conversation. Mitch offered her the phone but she drew in on herself and shook her head quickly. She was torturing herself over his dad and Ellen's exile. Mitch could all but feel her sadness and guilt. He brought her close.

He positioned the receiver so she could hear with ease. "Everything okay with you and Dad?" He'd been receiving regular updates so he knew they were safe.

"Oh, yes, we're fine. The detective boys are taking good care of us."

He smiled at Ellen's description of the formidable Rolando and Quinn. "I'm glad to hear it."

"I'm not sure where we are, but it's so pretty here. The boys have us in an older neighborhood with mature trees just like home. There's a beautiful garden out back that's blooming with flowers. But we miss home. We miss you and Shelby. I don't mean to rush you, Mitch, but do you know how much longer we'll need to stay here?"

"I'm working on that, Ellen. You and Dad should be back home soon."

"We love you both."

"Love you both, too."

"Mitch, here's your dad."

"Son?"

"Hi, Dad."

"I heard you telling Ellen that you're working on getting us back home. I'm not asking for details. I was a cop for twenty years and I know better. Since we've been here, I've done some reading up on Rossington. He needs to go down."

Mitch's lips flattened. "I'll make sure of it."

"We'll let you get back to work, son. Bye for now."

Mitch ended the call. Shelby's eyes were downcast. He tilted her chin up so their gazes would meet. "Okay?"

"I'll be better when they're safe and at home."

"Soon." He pressed a kiss to her hair.

Morales returned to the room, sipping from a can of soda and Mitch escorted Shelby back to their apartment. Inside, he went into the bedroom to retrieve an item from his suitcase and when he returned a few moments later, Shelby had resumed her perch on the end of the couch.

He sat beside her. He turned her hand palm up and placed her cell phone in it. The reason he'd taken it from her no longer applied. "You'll need this to call Sara while I'm gone."

"Thank you."

"Church and Morales will be taking turns staying in here with you. Another of my men, Detective Pearson, will be here sometime tonight to cover for my absence." Mitch framed her face between his hands. "I'll be back when this is all over, baby."

Shelby wrapped her arms around his neck. "Don't worry about me. I'll be fine. Just keep your mind on what you need to do."

Mitch crushed his mouth to hers in a thorough, deep kiss.

He'd left the front door open. Morales knocked softly on the frame.

Mitch kept his mouth on Shelby's for another instant then slowly drew back. "See you later."

Shelby nodded.

He released her and pushed to his feet. At the door, he said to Morales, "I'll be in touch."

"Yes, sir."

Mitch had no doubt she was in safe hands. Would not be leaving her otherwise. Now that the moment was at hand, though, it was hard for him to go. He paused at the door and closed his eyes, fighting back the need to be here to protect her himself. She didn't need him here now. She needed him to end this with Rossington.

Mitch left the apartment and took the stairs down to where his vehicle was parked.

* * *

It was the middle of the night when Mitch parked in front of his cabin in the Adirondack Mountains. He hadn't been up here in several months when Gage was living here. Stars lit the sky and the view was spectacular. While he couldn't help but appreciate the beauty, he wasn't here to sight-see. He'd chosen his cabin as the place to draw Rossington. He would be able to see a ground or air assault coming.

Mitch had called Harwick and left it to his detective to get the word to Rossington that Shelby was being housed here. Security was tight with his people stationed all around the place. He'd made no effort to make this look as if he and Shelby were alone. Rossington would expect that he wouldn't take chances with Shelby and to do less would shout set up.

Mitch turned to his police woman, Kelly McNamara, in the passenger seat beside him. She was newly promoted to detective and this was her first assignment in her new role. "Ready?"

Kelly nodded and the ponytail she'd looped through the back of his NY Mets ball cap bounced. Shelby had often worn that cap and that's why he'd chosen it for Kelly. He looked her over critically. Kelly had Shelby's build and coloring. With the brim pulled low, her face was shielded. Up close, she would never be mistaken for Shelby, but from a distance Rossington couldn't be sure and that lack of certainty would force him to move in for a closer look and then they'd have him.

"Stay inside the car until I come around to get you, McNamara," Mitch said. "If Rossington or his people are watching, we want them to see we're not taking any chances with you."

"Roger that, sir."

Mitch drew his weapon and walked quickly around to the passenger side. He'd parked the SUV as close to the cabin's front door as he could. Walters, the detective who'd accompanied him and Kelly, exited the back seat and together they formed a shield around her and hustled her inside.

The front door opened into a living room. The interior looked much as he'd last seen it with its worn leather couch and chairs, scuffed flooring, and light paneled walls. A short hall led to a kitchen and showed two closed doors, one for the only bedroom and the other for the bathroom.

The cabin had been the location of a showdown when Gage had been staying here with Mallory. Outside, the bodies and other indicators of the full-on assault Gage had faced were long gone. Inside, though, the cabin still showed some signs of the security measures Gage had taken. Though Gage had been back to the cabin after that, he hadn't completely set the place to rights.

The curtains over the large front window were

drawn. A towel was tacked to the window over the door. The cabin was in darkness. Mitch had heard from Gage that he and Mallory had lost power. Later, Gage made a repair to the generator and refilled it with gas. Mitch turned on his flashlight until he got the generator going and threw a beam into the room.

Gage had left wood stock piled by the door and the mattress to Mitch's king-sized bed, piled high with bedding, lay in front of the unlit fireplace.

Mitch walked around, making sure the cabin was as unoccupied as it looked. It was and with that done, he returned to the closed front door where he'd left Kelly and Walters.

"Stay here," he said to Kelly, "while Walters and I get our supplies out of the truck."

Not long after, the lights were on and the refrigerator and small chest freezer were humming. Hot water flowed out of the pipes and the heater had dispelled the chill in the air.

While Walters brewed coffee, Mitch checked in with the lookouts he'd stationed at various points up the mountain. "Any movement?"

"That's a negative, Chief."

"Okay. Turner out."

Mitch repeated the calls until he'd received similar responses from each. He checked his watch. Not long since he'd been in contact with Church and Morales, but he called them again.

Morales responded to Mitch's call. "Anything going on there?"

"Quiet here. Pearson arrived. He's on surveillance while I'm in with Dr. Grant."

"Call her to the phone."

"She went to bed about a half hour ago, Chief. You want me to wake her?"

Mitch blew out a long breath, feeling restless. "No. That's fine. Let her sleep."

He ended the call. He hoisted the mattress and returned it to the bed, then laid out fresh bedding for whoever decided to crash there. When he returned to the main room, he left more bedding on the couch.

Kelly and Walters were at the kitchen table, sipping coffee and playing cards. Mitch wasn't in the mood for games, but the coffee drew him. He took his cup to the hearth and built a small fire then checked in with Zach. All was well there. He expected it would be. He would have heard if there was a problem, but he was relieved to hear Zach confirm it. Since Mitch had taken Sara from the farmhouse, she'd dug a spot in his heart. He would see her safe and able to have a normal childhood.

Behind him, Walters yawned loudly and stretched. "I'm calling it a night. I'll bunk out on the couch. See you in the morning."

Kelly was taking first watch. Walters, second. Mitch, third. Mitch should get some sleep as well, but that didn't seem likely with his mind racing like a hamster on a wheel. He was feeling tight. He rolled his shoulders to relieve an ache there.

Kelly hid a yawn behind her hand. Mitch knew he wasn't going to be sleeping anytime soon.

"Get some rest, McNamara," Mitch said. "I'll take this watch."

CHAPTER FOURTEEN

Shelby sat heavily on the bed. She ended another call to Sara. Her little girl had gushed that she'd seen a 'wabbit'. Big news. Sara was bubbling with excitement. Shelby wished she'd been there to share the moment. *Soon.* She was clinging to that.

From her bedroom, she could hear the television in the living room. The volume was loud. Detective Morales was sprawled on the couch watching a reality show. He and Church had been taking turns staying in this apartment with her. Another night had fallen. Mitch had been gone for three days. She'd spoken with him and knew Christopher had not taken the bait. A shiver went up her spine as if her brother now stood behind her.

She fled the bedroom and joined Morales in the living room. A steaming mug of coffee sat on the table in front of him. The first of many, judging the other nights he'd guarded her.

"Mind if I watch with you for a while?" Shelby

asked.

Morales turned his heavy-lidded gaze on her. "Be my guest."

She sat down on the soft, plushy chair and focused on the television, determined to lose herself in the program. Morales was a man of few words and they sat in silence watching the people on the screen attempt one physical challenge after another.

Her phone rang. Mitch? After speaking with Sara, Shelby had left her phone in the bedroom. She sprang off the couch and went to the nightstand. Caller ID read Ed Turner.

Though Ed had been more kind to her than she deserved over this with Christopher, her nerves vibrated at the prospect of speaking with him. But she loved Mitch's dad and he obviously had something he wanted to say to her. *Don't be a coward.*

"Ed, hi," Shelby said.

"Hello, little sister."

Shelby sucked in a breath. Her heart stuttered then pounded like a jackhammer. "Christopher ..."

She dropped the phone onto the carpeted floor and recoiled from it as if it were a snake. Not a snake. Far, far worse. Her breaths quickened. Had Christopher found her? She shook her head. No. If Christopher had found her, he wouldn't be making phone calls. He'd be in this apartment with her. Then another thought struck her. What was Christopher doing with Ed's cell phone? Fear for Ed now had her snatching up her phone.

"What are you doing with Ed's phone? Where

is he?" She blurted out the questions.

"We're having a nice visit, Ed, Ellen, and I. Well, nice for me. Not as nice for them."

Shelby's throat constricted. "Don't hurt them."

"That's up to you. Did you really think I wouldn't find out you and Turner are at his cabin?"

Christopher really did think she was there with Mitch. But he hadn't gone there himself. He'd had another plan. Chills raced up her spine. "Ed and Ellen have nothing to do with you and me—"

"They do because you aired our family business," Christopher snapped.

She could feel his anger as if it were a living, breathing thing. Her heart rate jacked up. "Please, please don't hurt them for something I did."

"I have hurt them, but I haven't killed them. Yet."

Shelby closed her eyes. "Please ..."

"You beg so sweetly, Shelby. You always did whenever you forced father or I to teach you a lesson. You should never have defied me and turned traitor. I wouldn't have believed you'd fall for that cop. It seems you're in need of one final lesson."

Christopher's voice lowered to a harsh whisper. The hair on Shelby's neck prickled. "What do you want?"

"I've missed you. Come to me. Alone. Use any means necessary to get away from your police chief. If you bring him or anyone else, I will kill these people."

She heard the sound of flesh striking flesh

followed by a painful grunt and Ellen's choked, "Please, leave him be! He's not well!"

She knew Christopher hadn't hurt Ed to convince her he meant what he'd said. He'd taught her better than to ever doubt him. No, he'd hurt Ed simply because he could.

"Where?" Her voice came out thread-thin with remorse and fear.

"The free clinic. You have two hours to get there from the cabin. The Turners won't live one minute more."

Christopher ended the call. Shelby stood, trembling. *Two hours.* Her mind felt numb from fear. Her fear wouldn't help Ed and Ellen. She had to find a way to save them.

She wanted to call Mitch but Christopher's warning rang like a bell in her mind. *If you bring him or anyone else, I will kill these people.* She didn't dare call him. She wrapped her arms around herself to still the trembling. Think. *Think.*

Christopher had said this would be her "final" lesson. He was going to kill her. She knew he would want her death since Mitch found her out. They'd been coming to this point since then. She wasn't brave and she didn't want to die but she couldn't let Ed and Ellen be killed because of her.

She wasn't going to make it easy for her brother to kill her. She would not go out without a fight.

She heard Morales flipping channels. She swiped tears from her cheeks. Church would be sleeping but she had to get away from Morales. Morales and Pearson who was in the command room. How was she going to do that?

She certainly couldn't overpower them and she had no weapon. She winced. Even if she had a weapon, she couldn't bring herself to hurt them. She paced from bed to dresser and back again, her steps becoming more brisk as her agitation grew. If only Morales and Pearson would fall asleep on the job.

Shelby drew a sharp breath and stopped in her tracks. Her purse was on the dresser. She grabbed it and began to rifle through the contents. Her fingers closed around the bottle of sleeping pills Brock gave her.

She dropped the handful of pills into the pocket of the black pants she wore and went to the livingroom. Morales's coffee mug was on the table, now about half full.

Shelby scooped up the mug. "I'm going into the kitchen to make tea. I'll top that up for you, Detective."

Morales glanced at her. "Thank you."

Shelby filled the kettle and placed it on the stove. She took the carafe from the hot plate and poured coffee into Morales's mug. She added a sliver of ice to cool the drink enough for immediate consumption. As she palmed two of the pills, she felt a guilt, a hesitation. She shook off the feelings and plopped them into the coffee.

Rather than setting the mug on the table, she held it out to the detective. He'd be more likely to take a drink before setting it down. He did. His cheeks filled and he downed a mouthful.

She dropped two pills into a second mug for Detective Pearson. She remained in the kitchen, pretending to make tea, while she waited for the pills she'd given Morales to take effect. When the kettle whistled, she quickly turned off the stove.

Fifteen minutes later, Morales was asleep with his head bent at an angle over his shoulder and his mouth hanging open.

She picked up the other mug of coffee. Pearson was seated in front of the instrument panel when Shelby let herself into the other apartment. If he thought it strange that she was bringing him coffee, he didn't comment, but accepted the mug readily. Possibly, the young detective didn't want to risk offending the woman his boss was going to marry. Not knowing if he took cream and sugar, Shelby had placed both on a tray.

She held up the small ceramic creamer and matching sugar bowl. "How do you take it?"

"Just cream for me," Pearson said.

Shelby added cream then held the coffee out to him as she had with Morales. She smiled at Pearson expectantly. He took a drink.

"Good coffee," Pearson said after he'd swallowed. "Thank you, Doctor."

Shelby nodded and in an effort to hide her impatience and not hover, she left him. On her way out she passed the other bedroom where Church slept. The door was still closed.

In her apartment, Morales was now snoring softly. Her gaze riveted to the clock mounted on one kitchen wall. When another fifteen minutes passed, she grabbed her purse and locked the front door behind her. She headed back to Pearson. She needed to confirm that he was asleep and she needed the keys to one of the detective's cars.

Eyes closed, Pearson's head rested against the high back of the leather chair. Where did they keep the car keys? Shelby looked about wildly but couldn't see them. She checked Pearson's pockets carefully and came up with two sets of keys. One of them had a four leaf clover ornament attached to the ring along with what looked like house keys. The second held only one key and a tag with a car make and number issued by the Blake County PD. Shelby closed her fist around that key. Pearson's service weapon was in a shoulder holster. Shelby grabbed it and ran.

* * *

Mitch poured himself another cup of coffee. He put it to his lips but then set it down with a thud on the kitchen counter in an outward display of the frustration he was feeling. It was the middle of the night. He was on watch while his detectives slept. Outside more of his men guarded the perimeter but all was quiet. Three days and Rossington had not shown himself. Rossington wanted Shelby badly and he would have made an appearance by now if he were coming. Mitch's hand fisted. His plan had been sound. There was no way Rossington could have seen that he'd used a decoy. Had Rossington been tipped off by someone?

Something was up. Mitch pushed off the counter. He took the untraceable phone from his jeans pocket and called Harwick. As arranged, he left no message and would wait for Harwick to see the missed call and return it when it was safe to do so. As he returned the phone to the back pocket, Mitch's own cell phone rang. Morales.

"Turner," Mitch said.

"Chief, something's happened here."

Mitch's body tensed. "Shelby?"

"Dr. Grant is gone."

All of Mitch's fears culminated in that single sentence. "Gone?" The word came out choked.

"Yeah. She took off in our car."

"Say again," Mitch demanded.

"She gave me something. Drugged me. I was asleep. I took the night shift. Same with Pearson. While we were out of it, she left in Pearson's car."

"She left on her own? She wasn't taken?" Mitch all but growled the questions.

"No, sir. Like I said she drugged us. I'm thinking she must have put something in our coffee. She topped up a cup for me and Pearson said she took him a cup, too."

His detectives had been focused on preventing Rossington from getting in—not on Shelby getting out. What the hell was she thinking? Why would she leave? Where had she gone? Mitch's gut began to burn. If something was up with Sara, he would have received a call from Zach or his men. For some reason, she'd left the safe environment he'd provided for her. Anger rushed through him that she'd leave his protection and expose herself. But more than anger, he felt bone-deep fear that she was now vulnerable to her brother who would be watching for her to surface.

The departmental issue cars were equipped with GPS tracking devices. He hoped Rossington didn't already have her, that when they found the car, they'd also find her. "Track the car, Morales. Call me as soon as you have a read."

"Will do, Chief."

Mitch's phone beeped, signaling another call. Dispatch. Mitch disconnected from Morales.

"Turner," he said.

"Chief, hold please for District Attorney Canyon."

Mitch was in no mood for Derek. He was about to tell dispatch to refuse the call but they'd already put it through to him. Derek came on the line.

"Mitch?" Derek said.

"If this is about Shelby—"

"Mitch." Derek's voice dropped, became somber. "Hear me out."

"I don't have time for this."

"Mitch, the safehouse where your parents were was breached."

Mitch's mouth dried. "What?"

"Rolando and Quinn are dead."

Mitch bowed his head at the loss of the two good men, then raised it sharply. He asked the next question though he knew the answer. "My father and step-mother?"

"Your folks are gone."

Gone but not dead. Rossington hadn't killed them along with Rolando and Quinn. Mitch expelled the breath he'd been holding and gave himself a moment to take in that his dad and Ellen were alive. "How did this happen?"

"We don't know."

Mitch took a sharp breath. The how didn't

matter. His dad and Ellen were out there somewhere. He had to find them. If Rossington had wanted to send him a message, he would have killed them. He hadn't. Why? What possible use could they be to him?

Then it came to Mitch. Only one use he could think of and his gut churned. Rossington wanted Shelby. He hadn't been able to get to her. Did he plan to trade his dad and Ellen for her?

"Mitch, you still there?"

"Yeah." Mitch's hold on the phone tightened. "We have a time frame for when Rossington went into the safehouse?"

"Rolando called for back up when Rossington's people went in. That was four hours ago."

"Four hours." Mitch closed his eyes.

"They could be anywhere by now," Derek said.

But Mitch was betting he knew just where he'd find his family and Rossington himself. He ended the call with the DA without another word to the man.

He gripped the kitchen counter. Was it coincidence that Shelby left Morales around the same time that Rossington's people converged on the safehouse where his dad and Ellen were? His gut was telling him this was no coincidence at all.

His body went cold, in the grip of a fear he'd never known before. He wasn't going to get a call from Rossington with a demand to trade his dad and Ellen for Shelby. There was no way he would have agreed to trade her. He'd have found another way to save his family. Rossington had set the trade up with Shelby herself.

Mitch's phone rang. Morales. "What have you

got?"

"Our car's at the free clinic on Mason Street. What do you want us to do?"

"Stay put. I'll be in touch."

Mitch disconnected as he glanced at his watch. He had a considerable distance to cover before he'd reach the clinic. He called his office. He gave the order for an unmarked vehicle to drive by the clinic and confirm their car was there, then to drive on and report back directly to him.

Walters raised his head from the couch as Mitch ended that call.

Walters rubbed a hand over his mussed hair. "Something up?"

Mitch gave the detective a quick update.

Walters came off the couch. "Shit. What can I do?"

As Mitch was about to answer, his cell phone rang. It was the patrolman he'd dispatched to the clinic.

"Chief, this is Gould. I'm doing the drive by at the clinic. We have a confirmation on our car. It's parked in front of the clinic."

"Anyone in it?"

"No, sir."

Mitch ended the call. If Shelby was at the clinic, that had to be where Rossington told her to meet. Mitch faced Walters. "I'm going to mobilize a team. I need you to wrap things up here."

Walters nodded.

Mitch made the calls to have his team in place when he arrived at the clinic. Shelby was inside with that animal. His dad and Ellen, too. Mitch's heart felt squeezed in a vise. Rossington would not let his dad and Ellen go even when he had Shelby. She'd given herself up and Rossington would kill her. He'd kill them all.

CHAPTER FIFTEEN

Dawn was still hours away and traffic was light. Shelby drove quickly, alternating glances between the road and the clock on the car's dashboard. Was Christopher gauging the hour by the clocks on the walls at the clinic? Were those clocks in sync with this one? Even one minute behind his time would be too late. She gave another glance at the numbers, barely blinking in her fear of the passing time. Was she late? Had Christopher killed Ed and Ellen?

Her heart was loud in her ears as she came to a stop at the curb in front of the clinic. She turned off the ignition but left the key in it. The street was deserted. The houses opposite the clinic were in darkness. All was quiet as a tomb. She closed her eyes at that thought that brought with it another wave of fear.

She got out of the car, and dug her key to the building out of her purse. But when she reached the front door, she found she didn't need the key.

The door was uncustomarily unlocked.

She stepped into the small narrow corridor of the waiting area. A kitchen, small staff room and a washroom were in this part of the building. Her low heels tapped against the tile, telegraphing her arrival. That and the thud of the door as she closed it behind her. It was dark now with the door closed and she squinted, but even before her eyes had fully adjusted to the gloom, she heard her brother.

"In the basement, Shelby. Don't keep me waiting."

Perspiration slicked her skin. She reached back to her spine. Beneath the maroon blouse she wore untucked over her black pants, she felt the reassuring grip of the gun she'd taken from Pearson.

The door at the end of the hall that led downstairs was open. She hadn't been in the basement before but as she descended the steps, she saw it was a typical cellar with its concrete walls and floors. Bare bulbs hung from wooden beams that crisscrossed the ceiling, and made the area as bright as a sunny day.

Clutching the railing more tightly, she took in the rest of the room. An old burlap couch was in the center. Christopher sat against the back, arms outstretched, like a lord of the manor holding court. Every strand of his blond hair was in place. His Italian suit was cut to perfection.

Two men stood against the wall behind him. Another man stood over Ed and Ellen. They were on the cold floor. Ellen's back was braced against the equally cold wall with Ed's head in her lap.

Dried blood had caked in the deep grooves of his face and one side was bruised and swollen. Seeing him hurt, hurt Shelby as well.

Ellen's gaze fastened on Shelby and her eyes welled with tears. Silent tears. She made no sound as they trickled down her cheeks. Ed's dull eyes lit when he spotted Shelby, filling with anxiety and fear for her. He struggled to lift himself but only managed to rise onto an elbow. She wanted to go to them, to hold them in her arms as she did in her heart, but there wasn't time for that. She had to see them safe.

Ed's wheelchair was not in sight, but his cane lay at his feet. It would do.

Shelby looked away from Mitch's family and to her brother. His icy blue eyes fixed on her with an unwavering stare, tracking her, predator to prey. The image threatened to bring her to her knees, quaking in fear, but she fought it off and moving quickly, crossed the distance to him.

Christopher made no move to stop her. Given their history, she must be the last person he'd think would pose a threat to him. When she reached him, she bent over him, wrapping one arm tightly around his waist beneath the suit jacket, and gripping his belt. With her other hand, she drew the gun from her waistband and pressed it to his heart.

"I'm here, brother." She infused as much steel into her voice as she was capable of. "Now let them go. This doesn't concern them. Family business, after all."

"No," Ed said, his fear for her evident in his voice. "I can't leave you behind!"

Shelby didn't respond. If she did, she was afraid she'd break down and lose it. "Christopher, tell your man with the Turners to stand by the wall behind you with the other two. Tell him to keep a wide berth from me as he makes his way there. To walk where I can see him."

Anger ignited in Christopher's eyes and a muscle pulsed in his jaw. "Our little kitten has grown claws." His voice lowered to a deadly hiss. "I will kill you for daring this."

Shelby held his gaze, forcing hers to be rock steady, though all she could feel now was terror. "I'm dead anyway. I've accepted that." She cocked the gun. "Have you?"

Her brother stared at her. Something in her eyes must have convinced him that she meant what she said.

"Miller, to the wall behind me. Now. Turners. Go." Christopher bit out the words.

When all of Christopher's men were against the wall, Shelby said, "Tell your men to put their hands behind their head, fingers linked."

Christopher pressed his lips together briefly. "Do it."

As the men complied, Shelby addressed the Turners. "Ed, Ellen leave now. There's a gray car parked out front. Take it. The keys are in it."

"Ellen will go," Ed said, "but my dear I can't leave without you."

Shelby's throat closed and for a moment she couldn't speak. "No. Please, Ed. Please, just go."

She could feel Ed's indecision, could feel that he was torn, but it had to be this way or else her coming here was for nothing.

Ellen got to her feet. Finally, Ed allowed her to help him to his. She plucked his cane from the floor.

It was slow going as they made their way out of the cellar and when they did, they needed time to reach the car and drive away. Shelby's hand cramped from the vise-tight grip on her brother but she maintained her hold and pressed the gun harder into Christopher's chest.

When she heard the outside door close followed by the roar of a car engine, her breath whooshed out in relief. Ed and Ellen were safe. They would call Mitch. She needed to hold her brother off until Mitch got here.

One of the steps creaked. Shelby gasped and turned her head away from Christopher and to the stairs. A man was making his way down. She knew him. The messenger from the alley.

As she was taking in the messenger's arrival, Christopher's hand shot out, seizing her wrist. His eyes sharpened to lasers. He jerked her wrist hard, then twisted. Shelby cried out. He kept up the pressure long after he drove her to her knees and the gun clattered to the floor.

* * *

The team Mitch had mobilized to go into the clinic with him was already at the scene. He was almost there when his cell phone rang. Harwick. The call he'd been waiting for.

"Dan," Mitch said. "Where are you?"

"Mason Street Free Clinic. Just got here."

"Are you inside with Rossington?"

"No. I was doing another job for him elsewhere when I got wind of what was going down and got my ass over here."

Mitch had been hoping Harwick was inside. "My ETA is less than five minutes. Dan, I want you geared up to go in with me and the team."

"Yes, sir. Mitch, we have your father and mother here with us."

"What?"

"We found them inside the car Shelby took. They were about to drive away from the clinic."

They were alive. Relief washed through him. "Shelby?" His voice was strained.

"Negative on Shelby. She's still inside."

He was half out of his mind with worry over her and those three words threatened the little sanity he had left. "And yet dad and Ellen are with you?"

"They told us Shelby got them out. She surprised Rossington. Pulled a gun on him and held him off so your folks could get away."

Pearson had said she'd taken his service weapon. Now Mitch knew why. She may have gotten the jump on Rossington, but that wouldn't last and what would Rossington do to her when he regained the upper hand? Mitch's chest tightened. "I'm within sight of the clinic now. Stand by."

Mitch's team was waiting for him a short distance from the clinic. They'd set up in a location where they would not be seen by Rossington. That was likely no longer necessary. They'd lost their element of surprise. By now Rossington would expect that Ed and Ellen had made contact and would be expecting Mitch's arrival. Mitch prayed Rossington hadn't already killed Shelby.

The pavement shimmered from the earlier rain and the smell of the earth was strong in the air as Mitch joined his men. Harwick greeted him.

"My father and Ellen?" Mitch asked.

Harwick nodded. "I'll take you."

His dad and Ellen were in the back of one of the team vans. Mitch stepped inside and hugged Ellen. Her face was ravaged by tears and pale as the moon. When his father attempted to leave his seated position and gain his feet, Mitch gently set Ellen back against the seat and turned to him.

"Son," Ed Turner said.

Mitch's jaw tightened at the bruises on his father's face. Despite his injuries, Ed gave Mitch a bone-crushing embrace. Mitch returned it but Ed didn't hold on long. He drew back quickly.

Ed's gaze filled with fear. "He said he's going to kill her, son."

Mitch closed his eyes. When he opened them he clasped his father's shoulder. "Dad, you and Ellen need a medic, but if you can hold off a couple of minutes I need some information."

Ed clasped Ellen's hand. "We're fine, son. What can we do?"

Mitch looked into his father's somber gaze. "I need to know where you were being held and how many men Rossington has in there."

"Basement. Room below the stairs. Three men plus Rossington himself." Ed's eyes conveyed his urgency. "Mitch, hurry."

Mitch's heart rate kicked into overdrive. He

squeezed his father's shoulder once more, then gave the order for one of the unassigned detectives to take his dad and Ellen to Blake County General.

Mitch had ordered the blueprint of the clinic to determine their best point of entry. As the car taking his father and Ellen drove away, he bent over it.

"I need some light here," Mitch said. His voice was tense.

Harwick jogged to him and held a flashlight over the document. Mitch narrowed his eyes in concentration. A door at the back of the building led from the cellar to the alley. The door Joseph Bowden had used the night he'd taken out the trash to the Dumpster and come upon Shelby and Rossington's man.

Though Rossington would be expecting them, Mitch didn't want to go in where Rossington could see them coming and pick them off one by one. He rubbed a hand down his face. Another door led to the lower level from a side entrance. It opened into a boiler room. He traced the circuitous path of a corridor. That corridor led directly into the main room of the cellar and would provide the cover they needed. Mitch pressed his index finger hard against the blueprint.

He gathered his team. "This is it." He tapped his finger on the blueprint at their entrance point.

His people and Harwick were already outfitted with protective gear. Mitch put on gear as well, then outlined his entrance strategy and assigned positions. He looked at each man and the one woman in turn then said, "Move out."

Mitch took up his position by the door. Harwick flattened himself on the opposite side and the rest of the squad fell in behind Mitch and Harwick. Mitch eased the door open. The hinge didn't squeak and he said a silent thank you to Joseph who must have kept the springs oiled.

Mitch led the way in, his gun up. The boiler room was dark and he was glad of the night vision goggles. He moved through the room rapidly and then was in the corridor that would lead directly to the cellar.

He and his team moved soundlessly down the hall. Mitch expected to hear some noise as he neared the end, but all remained quiet.

He motioned his intent to move in to Harwick. After receiving Dan's nod, Mitch charged into the room.

The cellar was empty. Shelby, Rossington and his people were gone.

* * *

Christopher dragged Shelby into the alley by the wrist that he'd surely broken. She bit her lip at the pain and stumbled after him. The moon lit their path. It had rained earlier. Puddles of muddy water filled the cracked and broken ground. The smell of rotting garbage rose from the Dumpster. There was an eerie quiet and she could hear their every breath.

By now Ed and Ellen would have contacted Mitch. He would be on his way. Christopher knew that too and that's what had prompted him to leave the clinic quickly. She couldn't let him take her away. She had to remain here where Mitch could find her. A van was parked at the end of the alley. Christopher was taking her there. She couldn't let him put her in that van. Once he did, she was as good as dead.

"You won't get away this time," Shelby said, summoning courage to stall for time. "It's over for you."

He jerked her to a stop and seized a fistful of her hair, using his grasp on her to force her up on her toes. He fastened those reptilian eyes on her. "Little sister, we're far from over."

Shelby sucked in a breath at his painful hold. He squeezed her injured wrist. Her legs buckled and her knees hit the ground. She bent over, fighting the urge to vomit.

Christopher must have noticed how close she was to losing the contents of her stomach. His face went taut and before she might throw up on his Italian shoes, he released her.

"Miller." Christopher gestured to a man with a goatee. "Take hold of my sister."

Christopher stepped away from her and the man he called Miller grabbed her under one arm and hoisted her to her feet.

* * *

Mitch reached the door at the end of the cellar that opened into the alley. He could hear voices outside. Rossington and Shelby. He swallowed hard. *Hang on, baby.*

"Make this difficult and I'll kill you right here."
Rossington.

Shelby responded immediately, her voice trembling but defiant. "Go to hell."

Mitch felt pride in her courage but right now it terrified him.

"Hilroy." Rossington's words were harsh with anger. "Give me your gun."

Mitch's heart thumped wildly. Sweat dripped into his eyes and down his neck. Another few steps and he'd be there. Sweet Jesus, don't let him be too late.

He held up a hand and counted down three fingers. Gun raised, he pushed through the door and swung into the alley. Rossington was spotlighted by the moon, holding a gun trained on Shelby.

"Drop it, Rossington!" Mitch said in a snarl. "Or don't. I'd rather take you out of here in a body bag."

Rossington's eyes flared. His face pulled tight with rage, but he lowered the gun.

"Wise choice." Mitch inclined his head and one of his men rushed to Rossington and disarmed him. "The rest of you," Mitch called out, "drop your weapons and lay facedown on the ground. Now!"

Mitch counted four men, one more than his father had mentioned. He swept his gaze around the alley looking for others his father may have missed but there was no place for anyone to hide. A Dumpster butted up against the faded brick of the building, leaving no space to fit a grown man. A bush grew wild against the refuse container, but it was too small to adequately conceal anyone.

Rossington's men lowered their weapons as their boss had, then dropped them onto the wet and rutted asphalt. Harwick grabbed the man who'd held Shelby by the scruff of the neck. Another of Mitch's men slapped cuffs on him and led him away. Mitch's men converged on the alley and in short order all of Rossington's people were in custody.

Mitch tore off the night goggles, lowered his weapon and holstered it. His eyes were on Shelby, running the length of her, reassuring himself that she was unharmed. He started toward her. The most important thing in the world to him was to get to her, to touch her and have tangible proof of what his eyes were telling him.

He was intent on Shelby when he caught movement in his peripheral vision. Rossington grabbed the gun from the cop holding him and knocked the man to the ground with an elbow jab to the face.

Rossington's lips pulled back in a sneer and he raised the gun. "I won't be the only one who doesn't walk out of here, Turner."

Even as he reached for his weapon, Mitch braced, expecting Rossington to make his move against him, but to his horror, Rossington aimed his weapon at Shelby.

"No!" Mitch shouted.

He rammed into her with his shoulder, pushing her to the ground, just as Rossington's bullet hit his chest. The impact felt like he'd been slammed by a train. His eyes closed and he went down hard. More shots rang out. Men shouted.

Shelby screamed. Mitch struggled to breathe. To move.

"Mitch! Mitch! Oh, God, Mitch!" Shelby's voice was frantic.

He groaned and forced his eyes to open. "Shelby, stay down!" He shouted. Filling his lungs with enough air to be able to shout cost him, but he ignored the pain. *Rossington.* Mitch's heart drummed. He had to know Rossington was no longer a threat to Shelby.

He lifted his head and called out, "Harwick!"

Harwick was at his side at once. "Easy, Mitch. An ambulance is on its way."

Mitch didn't give a damn about an ambulance. "Rossington?"

Harwick gave a satisfied grunt. "Dead."

Mitch nodded and allowed his head to fall back to the asphalt.

Shelby crawled to him. She leaned over him, her eyes swimming in tears that dripped off her chin and onto his face.

"Mitch! Don't move!" Shelby's words were barely understandable, she was crying so hard.

"I'm. Okay."

She seemed not to hear him as she desperately pressed a hand to his chest.

He caught that hand, stilling her movement. "I'm wearing a vest." He took a breath. "Vest stopped the bullet." He inhaled once more. He hurt like hell. He must have cracked a rib or three but that was the extent of the damage. Her eyes were wild with fear. He stared into them. "I'm okay, baby."

Shelby's mouth quivered. "You're okay?"

Mitch reached up to cup her nape. "Just tell me he didn't hurt you."

Tears had left tracks down her cheeks and his heart clenched. Her beautiful eyes filled again. "He didn't hurt me."

Mitch reached for her other hand to hold both of them in one of his. When he saw the condition of it, he rose onto an elbow, clutching his chest. Her wrist was swollen and at an unnatural angle, clearly broken. He sucked in air through his nose sharply. He wanted to drag Rossington back from hell and take his time breaking all his bones.

Mitch cradled the back of Shelby's head and brought her to him, pressing her face to his neck. She wrapped an arm around him. He winced at the discomfort of her tight hold, but he wouldn't move her. As an ambulance screeched to a halt at the mouth of the alley, he pressed her closer.

CHAPTER SIXTEEN

Shelby stood over the queen-sized bed in Mitch's guest bedroom. Sara was asleep in the center, surrounded by pillows. Her little fingers were loose around the ear of a grinning stuffed rabbit.

Christopher was dead. Out of their lives forever. He was her brother, but Shelby couldn't grieve for him. For the first time in her life, she wasn't afraid. She was safe. She closed her eyes tightly. She was *free*.

With Christopher gone, and the threat to her and Sara removed, Zach had brought Sara back to her. Now, Zach was on his way out of the room.

Shelby looked away from Sara. "Zach. Thank you. I know I'm the last person you want to help right now."

He stopped walking and faced her. "Mitch would have helped you right from the start, Shelby. There wasn't anything he wouldn't have done for you."

Past tense and it drew blood.

"Mitch and I go all the way back. He's the closest thing I have to a brother," Zach said.

Shelby was surprised Zach had opened up even that much about himself. It was unlike him.

Zach's gaze remained on hers. "I feel for Mitch and what went down between you." Zach's tone had an edge, but lacked the anger and condemnation she'd been hearing. "That said," he went on, "what happened was between the two of you. I'm leaving it there."

She looked into his eyes. There was no anger in them, either. He nodded.

He turned away from her and resumed his departure from the room. She couldn't hear his footfalls and wouldn't have known he was moving if she hadn't been watching him. Zach, she'd observed, moved with the stealth of a cat and his presence wouldn't be detected unless he wanted it to be.

Without breaking pace or turning around he said, "Got some good news for you from Brock. The boy with the burns is out of the woods."

"That is wonderful."

"I'll be downstairs."

"Sara and I are safe now." Shelby shook her head. "You're staying?"

From outside the door he called back, "Still on the job until Mitch says otherwise."

Today Mitch was attending funerals for Sloane, Branson and Swartz who'd died in the car bomb. In two days, funerals would be held for Rolando and Quinn who'd been killed while protecting Ed and Ellen. Shelby wanted to be there with Mitch today to pay her respects to these men who lost their lives because of her and her brother. She'd stayed away, however. Members of the media had learned of her connection to Christopher and were camped out across the street from Mitch's house. Her presence would turn the funerals into a circus.

The blinds were down in this room to keep out prying eyes. Sunlight rimmed the edges casting a bright glow. The house was quiet other than the sounds of Sara's gentle breathing and the air conditioning clicking on and off. She planned to be gone from Mitch's house as soon as he returned and sent Zach on his way. The lease on her house was still in place. For now, she'd go there. This morning in all the chaos in the alley and then again at the hospital to cast her hand and treat Mitch's broken ribs, she hadn't asked Mitch to take her home but came back here to his house. But she couldn't presume he wanted her to stay.

She knew what she wanted—Mitch forever. After all he'd found out about her, and all that had happened between them, he may not want a relationship with her at all. Those thoughts brought pain that tore through her.

The door to the bedroom was ajar. It was pushed open the rest of the way. Shelby turned slowly, expecting Zach again. It was Mitch.

Her heart thumped as he joined her at the bedside. He looked like his usual self. If not for his careful movement, in deference to his sore ribs, she wouldn't have known he'd been hurt at all.

His gaze landed on her then went to Sara. "How is she?" He spoke softly and smoothed his finger tip gently across Sara's hand.

The tenderness in the gesture, in his eyes, squeezed Shelby's heart and made her wish for the impossible. That she could have come to Mitch with Sara from the beginning. What a wonderful father he would make.

Shelby's throat burned with a rush of tears. She swallowed several times then answered his question. "She's okay. Wonderful. Brock recommended a counselor for her. I don't think she'll need to see the therapist for long."

Mitch nodded. "I'm glad."

Shelby bit her lower lip. "I don't know how to thank you for all you've done. You gave me back my daughter." Her voice thickened. "You saved my life in that alley. You could have been killed." Her voice shook, recalling that moment he'd taken the bullet meant for her.

Mitch turned away from Sara to face Shelby and said gently. "I'm fine."

Shelby remained silent, beating back the terror. When she could speak again, she said, "Now that you're here and can relieve Zach of guard duty, Sara and I can give you back your guest room." She tried for a lightness she was far from feeling.

Mitch's eyes narrowed. "Where will you go? Back to France?"

She shook her head quickly, her hair swinging over her shoulders and back again with the strength of her denial. "No, that can never be my home again. I can never go back there again."

"Are you staying in Blake?"

"I'd like to." She licked her lips. "I'm not sure."

Staying in Blake without Mitch wasn't an option. To be close to him, to have her heart ripped out every time they had a chance encounter at some innocuous place like a grocery store, she couldn't do that. Or worse, to see him with another woman and have visible proof that he'd moved on. No, she wasn't into pain. She crossed her arms at the stab of hurt just the thought of him with another woman brought.

She linked her fingers and changed the subject. "With Christopher gone, you don't need my testimony anymore. And the FBI? They can't still be interested in speaking with me?"

Maybe she was into pain after all because her heart picked up with the hope that she would be needed here and would have a reason to spend some more time with Mitch.

"No. Your brother's organization is in collapse. We won't need anything from you." His gaze lowered to her hands and held. "You're still wearing my ring."

Shelby's fingers curled possessively over the ring for an instant before she willed them open. "I meant to return it. I hadn't planned on leaving with it. On keeping it."

"Is that what you want? To return it?"

His voice was strained, uncertain. Her pulse quickened. Was he questioning her feelings for him? She'd lied to him from the moment they'd met. She couldn't blame him if he thought her love for him was also a lie. Did he even want her love? Was that what his questions about the ring had been about? Or, was she reading too much into what he'd asked?

He was watching her with an intensity, a scrutiny that must be his cop stare. Nerves had her stomach flip-flopping. "No, I don't want to return it." She laid herself bare to him. "I want to wear it always. I've lied to you so much you must wonder how you could possibly separate the truth from the lies, but, Mitch, I never lied about loving you." Her heart was beating like a drum as she stared up at him, praying that he'd see the truth in her eyes and it would be what he wanted.

Mitch crushed her against him, mindless of his injured ribs. "God, how much I love you." His voice throbbed with emotion.

A sob broke from her and in a moment she'd be a blubbering fool but she didn't care. With one arm keeping her anchored against him, Mitch raised the other and took her face in his large hand. His mouth descended on hers, kissing her urgently, desperately. Shelby latched onto him, her fingers digging into his biceps, feeling that same desperation.

Sara let out a small cry and opened her eyes. Mitch smiled and released Shelby long enough to lift Sara from the bed and into his arms. Her little girl smiled back at Mitch. Watching him, her eyelids fluttered then closed and she fell back to sleep.

Mitch kept Sara cuddled in one arm and returned to Shelby. He wrapped her with the other. "Everything I'll ever want in this world is in my arms." His eyes burned with the force of his emotion. "Marry me, Shelby. There's no more reason to wait."

Shelby's throat tightened with happiness, with

love. So tight, she couldn't speak. She nodded vigorously. Mitch stroked her cheek, now damp with tears, and kissed her again.

TURN THE PAGE FOR A SPECIAL
PREVIEW OF KAREN FENECH'S NEXT
PROTECTORS NOVEL

HIDE

COMING SOON TO EBOOK
AND PAPERBACK

CHAPTER ONE

It was now or never. Allison Sandoval took one last glance over her shoulder. The ballroom was crowded on this Saturday evening, filled with the dignitaries and diplomats who'd gathered to honor her husband, Rafael, on his last night on U.S. soil. In the morning, he'd be flying back to his native South America. But he'd be leaving without her.

Rafael was tall and the height advantage gave him a wide view of the room, but the crowd around him was thick. Allison had been slowly working her way from his side. At any other time, it would be impossible for her to take more than a step away. He, or one of the men Rafael called her bodyguards but who were in reality her jailers, always yanked her back. But the men around Rafael tonight were as tall as he was and Allison took the opportunity to blend in with those milling around him.

Her grip on the champagne flute stretched the skin tight across her hands as she forced herself to move slowly, not to make a mad dash for the exit. She was sweating. Could feel perspiration trickling down her neck, left bare with her hair swept up into an intricate style, and continuing down her spine where the flowing silver gown cut deep to a "V".

At the door, an elderly man was making his way into the room. He held the door open and Allison breezed through it. With regret, she bypassed the coat check. The late October air was chill. She'd been out of the States for six months and in the South American heat, she'd forgotten how cool the nights could get in New York at this time of year. Didn't matter. She would not retrieve her coat. The place was crawling with security people who missed nothing. She could not risk anyone suspecting she was about to leave the building.

She'd almost reached one of the Ladies' rooms on this level of the luxury hotel. Earlier, when she'd accompanied Rafael on a tour of the building, she'd taken note of where the washrooms were located, seeking one that wasn't at the end of a corridor. What she'd found wasn't ideal, but she'd make do. She chose the restroom that provided the best access.

She turned down that corridor and kept walking. A door at the end of the hall led to a staircase. She made her way down the six flights. Her heels clicked against the steps, echoing in the stairwell, and she glanced back over her shoulder, fearing she would give herself away. But no one came charging through the door after her.

Rather than take the exit that opened to the lobby, she continued down to the underground garage. There would be a way to the street from there and freedom.

She dropped the glass of champagne she was still holding in a garbage can and left the hotel. The cold air hit her and while it stole her breath, it was also bracing. She was a long way from being free yet, but it was the closest she'd come since marrying Rafael. The last two months had been ... horrific. Tears sprang to her eyes. She blinked them back but some still fell. She swiped them away, angry with herself for going back there. For allowing Rafael to torture her even though she wasn't with him. She had been strong before. She would be again. She would not let that pain and fear defeat her. As hard as he'd tried, Rafael hadn't broken her. Her eyes stung with tears again and again she forced them back. Her life was not the only one that depended on her getting away from Rafael. She set a brisk pace down the street out of the lamp lights.

She needed a place to hole up for the night. A woman turned to look at her. Allison couldn't afford to be noticed, to have anyone recall she'd passed this way. She went into the shadows cast by the tall buildings and increased her step. She was breathing hard. She couldn't be caught. If Rafael found her ... For an instant, fear cut off her breath. No, she would not be caught and taken back to Rafael. She had to finish this with him. *She could not fail.*

She didn't know how long she'd walked when the tall buildings gave way to smaller structures spaced wider apart. Traffic, both pedestrian and vehicular, was thin here. One of the small buildings looked to be a business of some kind or maybe a small warehouse. Whatever it was, the place looked deserted for the weekend. The place would be locked but an alcove was dug into the building. It would cut some of the wind and the cold. Could she spend a few minutes there before moving on?

She ventured nearer for a closer look. No lights were on inside as far as she could see. Still, she hesitated. She couldn't afford to make a wrong move. If she came upon someone police would be called. Then Rafael. Fear had the back of her neck prickling. But the building really did look closed up tight. Allison was now shivering and huddling into herself in a futile attempt to get warm. She went as deep into the alcove as she could. It was dark and certainly not hot, but it did help with the wind.

A compact car pulled up to the curb. A man with thinning hair and a paunch that stretched the buttons of his thick overcoat dashed out. Leaving the car to idle, he jiggled a set of keys and made his way to a building across the street. Using one of those keys, he let himself inside.

Lights came on. Allison could see him clearly as he moved to a desk in the center of the room and opened a top drawer. He removed a brightly wrapped package, tucked it under an arm then dashed back to the door. He ran out and sped away in his vehicle.

He was there and gone in a couple of minutes. In his hurry, he hadn't turned off the lights. Hadn't locked the door. He hadn't even closed it, but left it to swing shut behind him. The door caught on something and remained partially open. Allison took a step forward. Her heart pounded. She looked up then down the street. A couple who looked to be in their fifties strolled by, then no one. Moving carefully, she stepped out of the alcove. Could she make it? Did she dare?

She crossed the street, moving quickly now. She was half-afraid when she reached the door, she'd find she was mistaken and it was closed, even locked. She couldn't always trust what her own eyes told her. She closed them briefly, afraid this would be one of those times. But, no. When she reached the door it was partially open. Her heart rate soared. She clutched the steel door knob and went inside.

* * *

Zach Corrigan was sleeping when the monitor beeped, signaling the secure perimeter around his house had been breached. He was instantly awake and on full alert. He rolled onto his side and punched buttons on the small panel in the wall, bringing up a view of the outside. He owned a large stretch of land at the end of Blake County, New York. Moonlight provided excellent light tonight, making the lights around the place unnecessary. Zach's house came into view along with the extension off the main house that served as the base of operations for his organization. The cameras he had set up at strategic points on the grounds showed several views of the place. Zach would see his visitors long before they reached his front door.

The vehicle making its way up the long

driveway was a limousine and though the occupant likely had no idea he or she was being monitored, there was no attempt to conceal the approach. An assassin wouldn't announce his arrival.

It was just shy of two in the morning on a Sunday. Zach's business didn't run nine to five and late callers weren't unusual. But if this were one of Zach's government contacts coming to his door about a mission, they would have called first. Zach's line of work made it essential that he be cautious. He made no apology for it.

He tracked the progress of the limousine. Decided to let it proceed. If he'd misjudged his visitor, he'd soon rectify that.

He slept naked and now put on jeans and a T-shirt. His gun was on his nightstand, always ready. He secured that at the small of his back, under the shirt, then left the bedroom.

A coffee maker was on a timer set to start at seven a.m. He got the machine going. As the rich aroma of the strong dark brew filled the air, the monitor beeped again, this time to indicate a presence on his driveway.

Zach called up the images on the kitchen monitor. Two men emerged from the limousine. One was built like a brick, clearly muscle for someone, but he stood against the hood of the black car, making no attempt to follow or shield the other man who moved briskly to Zach's front door and rang the bell.

Zach filled a mug of coffee for himself and drank a bit before going to the door to meet his visitor. He swung the door open and checked out the muscle. The guy hadn't moved from the limo. He stood with his arms folded at his chest, his hands tucked under his arms to ward off the cold.

Zach focused on the man in front of him. His cashmere coat flapped in the breeze. The wind put color in his cheeks that were sallow and drawn. His eyes looked heavy from lack of sleep. "Help you?"

"Are you Zachary Corrigan?"

Zach clocked the man at around his own age—early thirties. The guy had an accent. South American. Zach had spent enough time in that region to be able to pinpoint exactly where on the continent his visitor was from. This man was from a remote area. Zach had read in the newspaper about a diplomatic visit to the U.S. from the country's leader in a bid to secure financial aid. That leader was Rafael Sandoval, the man now standing here with Zach.

"I'm Corrigan," Zach said.

The man extended a gloved hand. The leather was of the finest, soft as melted butter. "I am Rafael Sandoval. Please, Mr. Corrigan. I need your help."

Sandoval's expression was earnest and desperate. Zach stepped back from the door and led the other man to the kitchen.

Zach topped up his mug. "Coffee?"

"No, thank you."

The man didn't look like he needed the caffeine. He looked about to jump out of his skin. Zach leaned back against the dark counter. In addition to jobs for Uncle Sam, Zach's organization also took on work from other countries and from the private sector.

"Roger Morse told me about you," Sandoval said.

Sandoval named one of Zach's government contacts.

"Though Mr. Morse thinks I need your aid for something developing in my country," Sandoval added. "He does not know the real reason I have come to you."

Zach narrowed his eyes. "Which is?"

"Before I begin, I must confirm that you are a military man."

Zach kept his gaze on Sandoval, wondering where this was going. "I'm sure you already got from Morse that I was a SEAL."

Sandoval nodded and let out a long breath. "I am also a military man. There is a code of honor among us. I need to ask for your utmost discretion."

"Why don't you tell me what this is about?"

Sandoval's shoulders slumped then he straightened his posture. "I need you to find my wife."

"I'm not a P.I." Zach wasn't going to elaborate on what his organization did. His contracts for the government were classified, sending him and his people into places in all parts of the world where others couldn't or wouldn't go. He maintained the same level of confidentiality for the jobs he took from private clients.

"I do not need an investigator," Sandoval said. "I need someone with your skills and your discretion. I am here in your country in an attempt to secure aid for mine. I cannot let word about my wife's disappearance become front page news. I cannot allow the focus to shift away from my country's very real need. This is a personal matter. My wife, Allison, and I were attending a reception in my honor yesterday evening. It was to be our last night in your country. We were to fly home this morning. One moment Allison was standing at my side and the next she was gone. I confess I was distracted. An agreement with your country would mean so much to mine." Sandoval rubbed his gloved hand back and forth across his brow with what appeared to be enough force to shred skin. "I wasn't paying enough attention to Allison."

Zach leaned forward. "If your wife was abducted—"

Sandoval squeezed his eyes shut so tightly the skin at the corners puckered. "No. She was not abducted. She left."

Zach pushed off the counter. "Unless your wife is a minor, she's perfectly free to come and go as she pleases. There's nothing I can do for you."

Sandoval rubbed his brow hard again. "Obviously, she is of legal age. You don't understand. She must be found."

Zach repeated his earlier statement. "I'm not a P.I. I can recommend a good investigator though I'm not sure you need one. You have your own people to look for her, my government and law enforcement would also look for her. You don't need me."

"My wife is delicate. Fragile. Law enforcement and government agencies would overwhelm her when they find her. She must be handled gently."

Sandoval withdrew his wallet and from it a photograph he held out to Zach. "This is Allison."

Zach glanced at the picture without taking it. The woman was a stunner. Waves of blond hair fell to her shoulders. Big eyes in a deep green rather than the blue he expected to go along with all that fair hair. She was dolled up and dressed to the nines in what looked like a pose for a State photo—wife of the country's new president. Zach raised his gaze from the picture and back to Sandoval. "This isn't the type of work my organization handles."

Sandoval ran a shaking hand back through his hair. "My wife is not a well woman."

The idea of an ill woman out on the streets without help didn't sit well with Zach, but if she were sick, why would she leave? There had to be a reason Allison Sandoval had left her husband. Zach eyed Sandoval and asked him straight out. "Why'd she leave you?"

"It was not deliberate. Allison wandered away from the ballroom last night. She does that if I don't keep a close watch on her."

Zach crossed his arms. "What aren't you telling me."

Sandoval's face drew tight in an expression of pain. "My wife suffers from delusions, hallucinations. She can't determine what is real from what is imagined. She is on medication but she has been gone since last night and has been without it. She must be found now. She won't survive long on her own."

Zach frowned. Clearly, the woman needed to be found quickly. He had no doubt he could do that and a lot faster than if he sent Sandoval on his way to find someone else to do the job. It wasn't his usual recovery mission but Allison Sandoval needed to be recovered. Zach addressed Sandoval. "I'll find her."

If you'd like to know when the next Protectors novel is released, sign up for Karen Fenech's notification-only newsletter at her website: www.karenfenech.com

Or type this direct link into your browser: http://www.karenfenech.com/books.html

Originally Released In Hardcover

Also Now Available As An eBook

GONE

FBI Special Agent Clare Marshall was separated from her sister Beth in childhood when their mother tried to kill them. Now Clare learns that Beth lives in the small town of Farley, South Carolina, but when she goes there to reunite with Beth, Clare discovers her sister is missing and that someone in the town is responsible for her disappearance.

Clare receives an offer to help with the search from fellow FBI Special Agent Jake Sutton. The offer is too good to refuse, though that is exactly what Clare wants to do. Jake is Clare's former lover, a man she cannot forget, and who has an agenda of his own.

Now while Clare tracks her sister, someone is tracking Clare, and finding her sister may cost Clare her life.

Originally Released In Hardcover

Available Now Also As An eBook

BETRAYAL

To save her son and people from a deadly enemy, Lady Katherine Stanfield marries her former betrothed, a man she'd betrayed but has never stopped loving. Katherine has never revealed her reason for the betrayal and now, five years later, believes her secret is safe.

Someone won't let the past rest. Someone with a secret of his own. She must stop that "someone" because he wants Katherine and her new husband dead.

ABOUT THE AUTHOR

PRAISE FOR THE NOVELS OF KAREN FENECH

{GONE} Karen Fenech's GONE is a real page turner front to back. You won't be able to put this one down!" —NEW YORK TIMES BESTSELLING AUTHOR KAT MARTIN

{GONE} "Karen Fenech tells a taut tale with great characters and lots of twists. This is a writer you need to read." —USA TODAY BESTSELLING AUTHOR MAUREEN CHILD

{GONE} Readers will find themselves in the grip of GONE as this riveting tale plays out. GONE is a provocative thriller filled with a roller coaster ride that carries the suspense until the last page." — DEBORAH C. JACKSON, ROMANCE REVIEWS TODAY

{BETRAYAL} "An excellent read." —DONNA M. BROWN, ROMANTIC TIMES MAGAZINE

{IMPOSTER: The Protectors Series - Book One} "IMPOSTER is romantic suspense at its best!" — USA TODAY BESTSELLING AUTHOR MAUREEN CHILD

{UNHOLY ANGELS} "... a superbly intricate tale of greed, power, and murder... a suspenseful and believable story that will keep you reading into the wee hours of the morning. Highly recommended! —BESTSELLING AUTHOR D.B. HENSON

Karen Fenech lives with her husband and daughter. To find out more, visit her website at: http://www.karenfenech.com

If you'd like to know when the next novel is released, sign up for Karen Fenech's notification-only news at her website: www.karenfenech.com Or, type this direct link into your browser: http://www.karenfenech.com/books.html

Made in the USA
Coppell, TX
06 April 2024

30995708R20134